A MEDICAL ANTHOLOGY

Comprising sixteen short stories spanning 100 years and covering many examples of good medical practice over the years, each story being a carefully crafted word picture of the clinical management at any one given time.

ISBN: 978-1-291-51325-7

By the same Author

A Complete Handbook for Professional Ambulance Personnel (1971)

John Wright & Sons Ltd. Bristol

Edward Jenner (1991)

Wayland

A Famous Nottingham Murder (2007)

Lulu

Additional Copies

Additional copies of this book can be ordered on line at the following address:

www.medicalanthology.co.uk

Acknowledgements

As ever I am truly grateful to the following persons for their considerable assistance to me in the preparation of this book, and not least their great patience in every particular:

My beloved daughter Mrs Stephanie North, and steadfast friend of many years Mrs Janice Woods, have between them worked through the 16 stories and other pages typing them from my manuscripts.

The business side of the work has, as usual, run smoothly due to the skills and dealings of my son Mr Philip Morris who has seen to the finer points and prepared the manuscript for publication with the company that has served me so well in the past.

Mr Philip Bird has provided the fine photograph of the Park Steps used on the front cover of this book. These steps lead up to what was the 'Private Residents' entrance at the rear of the former General Hospital buildings, at the top of Park Row, Nottingham. This image is also relevant to the '1958' story in this book.

Again I must thank my old friend Dr Paul Coe for his ongoing advice in respect with matters of 'Materia Medica'. Also Mr Chris Canner for his specific advice on the Cornish Riviera Express.

Lastly, as ever, I truly thank my cousin Dr Michael Cripwell MB BS DCH MRCGP for his usual wise advice whenever I was unsure of certain aspects of current general medical practice, plus all the horrendous change of recent years!

Notes Re-Photographs and Pictures

Most of the illustrations have come from my own collection, or as with the Hospital picture, from an approved source. The silhouettes were given to me many years ago by my step-mother from her own 1930's collection.

Contents

Dedication

This book is dedicated to the memory of my late Uncle, Dr Geoffrey Charles Morris, a much respected family practitioner.

Dr Morris came from a long line of doctors going back to the 1830s; several of whom initially studied at Lincoln College, Oxford, but when in 1854 St. Mary's Hospital in Paddington opened with a new Medical School, members of the Morris family wishing to read medicine were so inclined to study there in future.

Geoffrey Morris began his medical training in 1920 and was fortunate in that this coincided with the arrival at St. Mary's of the man later to be given the title of the 'Great Dean', Dr Charles Wilson. Perhaps he is now better remembered as Lord Moran (Churchill's physician).

St. Mary's was not in good shape when Dr Wilson began his role as sub-Dean in February 1920, but by the time my uncle arrived things were already looking better, with more students making application; some would be clinical students who had studied the pre-clinical course at Oxford or Cambridge and had passed parts I & II of the Second M.B. examination.

Clinical teaching at St. Mary's has always been good, and thus my uncle went through the whole five year course tutored by such men as Sir William Willcox, a fine physician and Forensic Analyst. On the surgical side there was Prof. J.E.S Frazer the great Anatomist and Sir Zachary Cope noted for his work on 'the acute abdomen'. Sir Almroth Wright was the famous lecturer on Pathology and Bacteriology; and of course the name most known, Sir Alexander Fleming, whose laboratory looked over the portals of the 'Fountains Abbey' public house (now I fear no longer), which would have been frequented by my uncle and his contemporaries!

For the youngsters today, Alexander Fleming was the clever young man who returned to his laboratory after a humid summer holiday to find some Petri dishes with an unexpected mold growing there. This was literally the birth of penicillin (so rarely prescribed today for various reasons, conveniently given! But it remains a good antibiotic, and not expensive!)

Dr Morris qualified with the London Conjoint Diploma M.R.C.S (Eng.) and L.R.C.P (Lond.) in 1925. Later, after various House Posts at St. Mary's and Queen Charlotte's Maternity Hospital under Mr A.W. Bourne, he experienced some General Practice locums in Wales and Yorkshire.

In the late 1920s my uncle held hospital posts in Psychiatric medicine, gaining the D.P.M. at Leeds in 1931. I don't know all the jobs he held, but amongst them was E.N.T. work at which he was very good, and he also had a great interest in anaesthetics. These interests stood him in good stead in subsequent General Practice work at Ravenglass in Cumbria and lastly, for well over thirty years, in the Lincolnshire Wolds, as a practitioner, who also did all or much of his dispensing. Here I knew him best.

In his time my Uncle was always a source of help to me and gave good counsel in my literary endeavours and otherwise.

Geoffrey Charles Morris was a fine doctor and although I was a nephew, in difficult times he was always there for me. I still miss him greatly.

Preface

Over the last 50 years I have much enjoyed writing on the many and varied aspects of what is today termed 'medical science'; originally considered to be 'an art'.

Many famous figures from the pre-Christian era contributed to early medical knowledge, yet the man given to represent medical learning is Hippocrates, said to have been born in the year 460 B.C. who came to be the 'Father of Medicine'.

Much about this celebrated man is very vague, but he is best known for the 'Oath' he devised, thus laying down a set of rules that had to be obeyed by anyone wishing to practice the art of Medicine.

History tells us that Hippocrates had no true knowledge – nor would he. Indeed he knew little of physiology, and pathology was also little understood in his time. Surprisingly he did leave some observation of what must have been pneumonia and also epilepsy, yet this latter seems to have been thought more the 'visitation' of a God!

In the 1960s when I was taking an active interest in Clinical Medicine, I came across the splendid books of Professor A.E. Clarke-Kennedy MD. FRCP., a Fellow of Corpus Christi College, Cambridge, also Physician to the London Hospital and formerly Dean to the Medical School.

The books that pleased me so were titled 'Medicine in its Human Setting' to be followed by 'Patients as People'. Both were published by Faber & Faber. They were illustrated by wonderful line drawings by Sylvia Treadgold, MSIA, Medical Artist from Guy's Hospital.

Professor Clarke-Kennedy told his clinical stories by creating what he so accurately called 'disease characters' who are likely to be seen on hospital wards and in the Clinics; and not less are to be found in the G.P's surgery. Each case gave an excellent lesson to the reader. They certainly left an impression on those who troubled to 'warm to them', be they newly appointed House Officers, particularly pre-registration 'lads and lasses' or others about to sit exams or who are summoned in the dead of night!

Finally, I can say that the stories in this book are all based on events both true and fictional. However what remains very true is the application of good medicine; whatever the form, and in which year matters little.

Into each story has gone care and indeed love, with the hope that the reader will feel the warmth of the tale.

The 'ART' is portrayed herein.

Stephen Morris
Elston
Nottinghamshire

Doctors apparently consider heavy drinking to be more than four pints of beer, four doubles or a bottle of wine a day. I should think that to be the national average lunchtime consumption!

Jeffrey Bernard

1910 – A Cough in the Park

When Nanny Watkins replaced Nanny Grayling in Alice's life, the four year old girl wept tears of anguish into the fur of her beloved teddy bear Cecil.

While kind, Nanny Watkins believed in a strict daily routine. Nanny Grayling had been so kind in other ways – the occasional hug, and listening to the worries of a little girl. She had also been very good when Alice was poorly. Nanny Watkins was not so tolerant of aches and pains. Not so patient with tummy-aches or runny noses. And one thing she insisted upon regardless was the mandatory walk in the park. Come rain or shine, the daily walk was a 'must'. Fresh air was what little girls and boys needed. If Alice felt poorly on her walk, Nanny always claimed it was 'all in the mind', and she was told to take deep breaths. In truth this was rather an odd thing for a Nanny to insist upon. Children of four were notorious for picking up germs that made them ill. Only obvious high fever ever seemed to draw Nanny Watkins attention to the infant complaint.

Winter was turning into spring; a pleasant day, yet Alice was snuffling, sneezing and giving the odd cough. Nanny marched her onwards through the park. The matter of deep breaths was urged, yet it made things worse. As they were passing a hedge with a gate into a private garden, an elderly man came out and Alice smiled at him and greeted him despite her woes.

The man was known to Alice but not to Nanny Watkins, who dragged Alice on impatiently. "Come along child" she chided, but the old man spoke to Alice in a most gentle voice - "Hullo my dear". Nanny glared at him. He addressed her. "May I introduce myself Nurse? I am Dr Penny, an old friend of Alice here". Alice sneezed loudly. Nanny Watkins was not pleased. "Handkerchief child!" she said. Then turning to Dr Penny, who was obviously looking closer at Alice with his head on one side, Nanny replied. "I apologize Dr Penny. Alice should know better." The doctor paused and asked if he could place a hand on Alice's forehead.

"Yes, naturally, if you think it necessary, but I think she only has a snuffle."

"I am retired now" the doctor said. "Who is Alice's new doctor?

"The family tend to consult Dr Jacob these days, yet I believe he is away at the moment."

"Then I suggest you take Alice home immediately, Nurse, and put her to bed. I will ring her mother and pay a professional visit within the hour. I do a lot of locums still. And I think she needs a doctor to look at her. Under the circumstances 'gratis' of course, as I am her old doctor."

Reluctantly Nanny Watkins walked Alice back home. She was relieved but Nanny was now very grumpy. Alice would like to talk to dear Dr Penny again. Tell him how she really felt. She was feeling very poorly by now.

Back home Nanny Watkins complained bitterly to Alice's mother about the casual meeting with Dr Penny and his over-concern and interference. Alice's mother explained that she had just taken a call from the doctor and said she was indeed glad that the old man had kindly offered to call and see the child as Dr Jacob was away. Dr Penny had brought Alice into the world and was wonderful with babies and young children; indeed he was thought to be wonderful with all his patients. If he felt Alice would benefit by his check on her there would be a good reason in his mind for it.

No sooner than Alice had been put into a warm bed there came a ring at the front door and there stood the old doctor now carrying his well known battered black Gladstone bag.

Dr Penny took a chair and sat by the bed. Nanny Watkins began to describe what she thought a minor ill – a slight chill – in a way that Dr Penny thought dismissive of something that so easily could be the early sign of one of the host of infectious diseases which could strike a little child of Alice's age; but he would, as always, have to be understanding and diplomatic for surely Nanny Watkins was a qualified children's nurse. "Are you going to let me have a look at you Alice?" he asked with a smile, at the same time gently taking the rather rapid pulse of a patient already feverish.

"Yes, if you don't hurt me" was the tentative reply.

"I would never do that my dear" smiled Dr Penny, his bushy white eyebrows raised in mock surprise.

Alice could have been symptomatic of any one of several infections. She was certainly full of cold, and had some distressing nasal catarrh. Dr Penny turned to Nanny Watkins and asked rather pointedly "Has Alice had any productive cough?"

Nanny answered that there was in her opinion 'nothing to speak of'. Again the doctor felt this a bit too dismissive of what could be an important symptom. He removed from the bag a stethoscope with the long red tubes and a conical metal chest piece. "Now Alice, you cough and I will listen." Alice produced a slight grin. "Is that bit at the end cold?"

Dr Penny laughed. "A bit perhaps, but I will warm it up for you dear." Nanny interrupted "Don't be silly Alice. Doctor knows best!"

There were few chest signs, but Dr Penny knew if he was right in his possible diagnosis a 'paroxysmal' cough would set in fairly soon. He hoped he was barking up the wrong infectious tree, but years of experience of little chests had at this stage hinted at what he was thinking. There was a fair chance Alice was in the early stages of whooping cough – pertussis – a serious childhood infection that needed prompt action and all the care he could give, were there to be a happy outcome.

Dr Penny then also examined Alice's mouth and throat. The whooping cough or pertussis bacillus had been isolated only four years previously and was known to be abundant in the phlegm produced in the early stages of the illness. The doctor planned to take a swab on his next visit, but now looked for a key diagnostic sign – a small ulcer under the child's tongue. Unfortunately there was one clear to see.

Dr Penny was firm with Nanny Watkins. "Alice must stay in bed with the room well ventilated. She must be kept quiet and comfortable, and I must be informed immediately if she shows signs of coughing and a 'whoop'."

Nanny went pale. Dr Penny continued "I am sure you have nursed such a child patient before? We have found the infection early, so can carry out such treatment as we have."

Nanny Watkins pursed her lips and seemed none too pleased. She still felt this was all a bit presumptuous by the retired doctor. A younger, more modern man might be better. Nor did she give Dr Penny a direct answer to his question. She had in fact only seen one infant with whooping cough. And the outcome had been unpleasant, swift and fatal.

Dr Penny descended the staircase and was welcomed by Alice's mother Mrs Penby-Jones. "Come into my morning room Doctor. I would value your views and advice on little Alice!"

Dr Penny was worried on various counts. At this stage in the illness how much should he say to the child's mother? He also had his reservations about Nanny Watkins' ability. She had not asked a single question of him, and seemed a frightfully cold woman. At the moment he knew that careful speech was essential. The next day or so would clarify matters. Any immediate deterioration would entail Alice's removal to the isolation hospital, fortunately but a short distance into town.

"I want you to be totally honest with me Dr Penny" said Mrs Penby-Jones. "Just how ill is Alice?"

Dr Penny took a chair and said quietly "Alice has the symptoms of what – at this stage – could certainly be whooping cough. But in truth many of the expected symptoms have not yet appeared. I will, I am afraid be a very regular visitor over the next forty-eight hours. And will be with you immediately should you call me."

Mrs Penby-Jones was silent for a moment. "I wonder" she said "Should I get a children's nurse in? Miss Watkins is, in confidence, not the best children's nurse. Good as a nanny, but..."

"I tend to agree that a specialist fever nurse would be best" replied the old Doctor. "I will arrange for one to come down from the isolation hospital within the hour. I take it you will tell Miss Watkins? But keep her to hand."

Leaving the Penby-Jones' house on the Park Estate, Dr Penny cycled – as GPs did in those days – round to the Isolation Block of the Children's Wing at the General Hospital, on what was Postern Street near the Castle. He was welcomed as an old friend by the Children's Sister in Charge. "My dear Doctor Penny, I quite thought you had hung up your stethoscope for good" she laughed, "but it is lovely to see you. Do you have a little patient for us, or do you wish to 'borrow' one of my girls?" They sat in Sister's room and sipped coffee. "The latter, if you would be so kind Sister, for a four year old girl in the Park Estate. Her Nanny may need help. I fear the child has whooping cough, although I am still waiting for a definite whoop." He smiled. As usual Sister thought "What a lovely man. This City owes him so much!"

"The child is Alice Penby-Jones, a little dear."

Sister was shocked. "Why, Mrs Penby-Jones is a Member of the Linen Guild over at the General Hospital. A charming family, as you will know Dr Penny. Yes of course we will find a nurse for her. Matron will be most concerned. Would you rather have Alice come straight to us?

"No, it's a shade too early. 'Pro-tem' the cough is non-paroxysmal, but I am going back after lunch to take a swab and drop off a bottle of expectorant mixture in case things begin to happen in the night."

And so arrangements were made and Dr Penny made his way home for a late lunch.

* * * *

When the Doctor's cook/housekeeper heard his return, she took his meal out of the oven. It was in remarkably good shape, for Mrs Prince was an old hand at providing edible meals long after the time they should have been eaten. Mrs Prince had been with Doctor Penny for nearly fifteen years, both before and after Mrs Penny had died of pneumonia in the spring of 1900. Had it not been for this faithful soul she was sure the Doctor, even though semi-retired, would forget to eat and rest if busy. Medicine was his vocation. He had always been busy and his patients loved him.

He apologised to Mrs Prince and did her offering justice, yet all the time thinking about little Alice and possible developments in the hours ahead. He was however pleased he had made an early move about getting in a specialist paediatric 'fever nurse'.

* * * *

A ring at Doctor Penny's surgery door came as he was having a cup of coffee after his luncheon. Mrs Prince ushered the caller into the 'lonely' surgery – for it was hardly used now – then she went into the dining room. Apparently the caller was the fever nurse from the hospital en route to the Park Valley. Sister had suggested that as he lived so close she have a word with Doctor Penny and get herself briefed about her assignment. And she had with her a large bag of equipment to set up for such a case. She was Miss (Nurse) Wilmot. A tall girl with a pleasant manner. As soon as he saw her, the Doctor knew she would be good at her job, and good with Alice Penby-Jones.

"You will like little Alice" Dr Penny smiled. "She is a good little soul. I should however say a word about her Nanny, a Miss Watkins. She is what one would term rather 'a cold person'. I have observed her manner with Alice and she was too impatient with the child. I do not mean this unkindly; it is just an observation based on years of medical practice."

The Nurse blushed and seemed touched by the hint of confidentiality between doctor and nurse. Doctor Penny was clearly a man she could work with. "I presume you want me to take prime care of the case?"

Dr Penny smiled. "Of course" he replied. "As you know, Nurse Wilmot, the treatment of whooping cough constitutes the reproaches of the art of medicine. There is no true method of shortening the disease. All we can do is guide the case to recovery, modifying symptoms, watching for complications and – particularly in your part – making our little patient as comfortable as possible. Although we are in 1910 there are as yet no specifics to be found. I will call Mrs Penby-Jones and tell her you are coming to organise things in the sick room and also assess the child. I will arrive about four thirty and bring with me the first bottle of medicine in the limited armamentarium from my dispensary. Now be pleasant to Nanny Watkins and enlist her help generously. You will soon be able to tell if she is truly competent, for I may be doing her an injustice. There my dear I will let you get on your way." He smiled warmly. Nurse Wilmot knew they would get on well together.

* * * *

After a brief 'nap' (one of Mrs Prince's 'standing orders'), Doctor Penny made his way to the dispensary to mix up two bottles of medicine for Alice Penby-Jones to begin her treatment as such as it could go 'pro tem'

The Doctor was strangely fond of his dispensary – a narrow room with a stone floor that led off the surgery. It was a room of distinctive smells – antiseptics and iodoform/liquid and powder; the sedative paraldehyde; sour valerian; ether and chloroform and many more of his tinctures and stock medicines in their big fluted bottles. All was orderly and neat, and on a small table especially for the purpose, was the white wrapping paper, red sealing wax and matches. There were also pill boxes of different sizes and colours. A pen and ink stood by for the Doctor's instructions to be written. The dispensing ledger was also to hand.

As yet Alice had not entered the paroxysmal coughing stage of her illness, but he would dispense a suitable expectorant to help her in this early stage. He went to another long shelf and selected a 'four fluid ounce' paediatric medicine bottle with its cork.

Amongst other ingredients the mixture contained carbonate, chloride and acetate of ammonia, plus syrup of squills, potassium iodide and spirits of nitrous ether. It sounded nasty, but each ingredient was miniscule and the mixture known to be very effective in this early stage.

Nurse Wilmot was expected and arrived at the Penby-Jones home in the afternoon – but of course not in the middle of tea! She was welcomed willingly and indeed the hospital in the person of her Ward Sister had telephoned in advance to give a reassuring verbal reference, promising a written one to follow.

Alice had been put to bed by Nanny Watkins who was, it appeared, rather diffident about the turn of events, nor had she seemed too enthusiastic or grateful at the announcement of a specialist 'fever nurse' coming onto her territory. Indeed, she was still of the opinion that the chance meeting with Doctor Penny had set in motion too much fuss and palaver over an infant's cold and snuffles.

Nurse Wilmot was very polite and friendly to Nanny on meeting her, sitting privately with her in 'Nanny's room', discussing the situation and saying how fortunate it was that Doctor Penny had seen Alice and Nanny on their walk and noticed the rising fever. Just then the door-bell rang and the house-maid greeted Doctor Penny – back as promised. As Alice was in a fitful sleep Mrs Penby-Jones, the nurses and Doctor Penny held a little discussion on immediate action. Firstly he had a quiet look at his patient again and noted her body temperature by placing the flat of his hand on her bare abdomen. Alice opened her eyes and gave him a 'wan smile'.

Doctor Penny smiled back, saying softly "We have an extra nurse come to help you get better Alice dear. Nurse Wilmot. She works especially with children who have illnesses like the one you have." He beckoned for Nurse Wilmot to take a chair next to the bed. "We will all make your bedroom into what is a little private, one-bed hospital. Nanny and Nurse will be with you night and day until you are free of your 'snuffles' and that cough that sounds as if it is getting a bit more troublesome. I will call every day, or more often if you want me. I want you to get truly better." Suddenly Alice started a long bout of coughing in what were short sharp paroxysms which ended in a great whoop. Then she was sick into a bowl Nurse Wilmot had quickly taken to hand. Alice fell back on her pillows exhausted; pale and rather blue round the lips and ear lobes.

The Doctor sounded her chest and hardly without her noticing took a swab in its tube from his pocket and wiped a sample of the mucous in her mouth. "I will take this to the hospital laboratory straight away." He labelled the tube and put it in his bag. Then he removed the small bottle of medicine that he had brought with him. "Start Alice on a full dose of this immediately, please. It would seem she is well into 'pertussis' already, so give her the full nursing regime please Nurses."

As the Doctor went downstairs he could hear the professional patter of nursing feet as the rooms were adapted to the sick-quarters. Nurse Wilmot's big nursing bag had all the gear therein.

* * * *

With Nurse Wilmot's constant calm reassurance, Nanny Watkins became less apprehensive; more sure of herself. She was really a good 'General Nurse', fully qualified, but had not had much paediatric experience, leaving hospital work to become a Nanny when she had enough qualifications to secure such an appointment. She was fond of children yet her strict upbringing had rubbed off on her. Working alongside Nurse Wilmot had influenced her and brought out her gentle side. She eventually felt she could confide in her new colleague.

"Nurse Wilmot, I feel I have been rather off-hand with you. Indeed you came as a surprise. On reflection I am actually very relieved and glad to be working with you" she smiled. "You are a good paediatric nurse. Anyone can see that." Nanny Watkins meant every word.

* * * *

The two nurses cleared Alice's room of furnishing that was not needed and carpets that could be vomited on. A nursing table was placed under the window from which came adequate ventilation. And the 'vaporizer' gently emitted its helpful medicated steam. Alice was more comfortable than she had been for a while. However it was early days yet. The coughing, whooping and vomiting would continue.

The nurses wanted to remove Alice's favourite Teddy Bear, but Dr Penny had plans for him!

Back home Dr Penny had tea, then went to his dispensary again. He had something special to prepare to make Alice feel happier.

It had really been very fortunate he had met Alice and Nanny Watkins as he entered the park by the garden gate. He hoped that his final visit of the day to the Penby-Jones house would find his young patient easier and certainly no worse, but she was still a long way from 'well'. And years of dealing with children had taught him that when they had a fever and had to be parted from a loved toy they would be sorrowful. He thought of Alice's teddy bear and so went ahead and prepared some protection for him! This was a mixture of thymol, creosote, caryophylli and ether; 10 drops of each substance all made up in a small 'fluted' green bottle – labelled 'for Mr Teddy Bear'. Nurse Wilmot would know to dab it generously on poor old Teddy and thus Alice could have him back on the little table by her bed, and when she got better begin to hold him again. A simple thing to do, but if it made a small child better…worthwhile a procedure.

Nanny and Nurse Wilmot had got Alice to drink a little barley water at tea-time, but after another bout of coughing and the inevitable whoop, she brought it back up. Her temperature had risen and her heart and pulse raced. The Doctor arrived at 6.30, fortunately bringing with him a mixture to reduce the whooping and which contained amongst other medicaments, 'bromoform' and 'spirit of chloroform'. He had to reduce the whooping and add sedation to the treatment.

* * * *

Doctor Penny heard Alice begin another bout of coughing as he opened the bedroom door. A rapid series of expiratory coughs made the child's face become blue and bloated, then came the whooping through the partially closed 'glottis', the space between the vocal folds or cords. Following the last whoop as expected Alice vomited again the sticky mucus.

Something had been nagging at the Doctor's mind – still sharp after so many years in family practice. It had been said that Alice had only suffered mild symptoms from the previous morning. And of course she had been in the Park that morning when Doctor Penny had seen her as he came through his garden gate. But she must have had symptoms worsening over a few days, not just a snuffley cold as mentioned by her Nanny. Had Nanny Watkins, with her brusque manner just brushed aside the 'grizzling' of a 'feeling poorly' child? Yet Alice had never seemed to him to be a child who complained unnecessarily.

The result of the swab Doctor Penny had dropped into the hospital laboratory at tea-time came through before the evening was out. The result was clearly pertussis. He now knew he would have to question Nanny Watkins more carefully on the time sequence of the child's illness. He still sensed a resentment of him for some reason he could not fathom out. Nurse Wilmot had not presented a problem and the two nurses seemed to be working well together. It must be something that happened in the past that posed the problem.

Nurse Wilmot gave a clear and short report. The worry was not just the fever but the effect on Alice's heart of repeated coughing and whooping. Her face was so cyanosed and her tongue protruded. She also had bleeding in the whites of her eyes termed conjunctival haemorrhages. There were also nose bleeds. All-in-all a ghastly clinical picture. And there had certainly been deterioration since the morning.

"Did you notice anything amiss with Alice earlier this week?" the Doctor casually remarked, putting his stethoscope into his bag after listening to the infant chest. Nanny Watkins looked taken aback. Hesitantly she replied in a low voice "Perhaps Alice has been off her food and rather quiet. But I assure you there has been no temperature or real sign of cough or cold."

Doctor Penny gave her a knowing look, then he smiled. "I see. Well her heart sounds as if it can cope. I have two bottles here in my bag. One is a mild sedative for Alice to have at night. And one is for your Mr Teddy." He spoke directly to the exhausted child. "Now I know Nurse has had to move him into another room, so in case he has caught your nasty illness here is a little bottle all of his own which can be dabbed on him and in a day or two he can come back to you. How's that?"

Alice managed a little smile, but started coughing again. When the paroxysms had passed, Nurse Wilmot prepared a dose of the 'night' medicine. And the Doctor stroked Alice's forehead; left his final instruction with the Nurses and left the room to go and give his report to Mr & Mrs Penby-Jones.

* * * *

Doctor Penny was greeted in the Drawing room by Mr and Mrs Penby-Jones. They were dressed for dinner, but in no hurry for they urged the Doctor to take a glass of sherry with them. He accepted and then prepared to answer their questions on Alice's progress, yet could not in truth be sure of the prognosis at this stage. Mrs Penby-Jones asked him to be frank with them; not keep anything back.

He said "This evening Alice seems to be, should we say, stable. Her temperature is still raised, but not dangerously so. And her chest is as I would expect it to be. The coughing is very distressing naturally, but there are no signs that her heart is weakening."

As he paused for breath and reflection Mrs Penby-Jones asked the obvious question every doctor comes to expect at this juncture.

"Is there a chance of Alice not surviving this most dreadful illness Doctor Penny? I have seen it before. My dear brother Harold was taken by it at an early age." Her words were hushed. Doctor Penny reached out and took her hand. "A Doctor must always remain optimistic, unless of course the patient is clearly moribund. And even then he has to keep hope in his heart. Where Alice is concerned, having seen her this evening she appears to be responding to treatment. If you wish I would like to make one further call between ten o'clock and ten-thirty, just to see if she needs anything stronger to settle her for the night." The Doctor paused to sip his sherry.

Mr Penby-Jones turned to his wife and nodded, then told Doctor Penny he must do whatever he thought best. "You are very kind Doctor. I will wait up for you." They shook hands.

As the old Doctor cycled away from the mansion in the Park Estate, he prayed all would end happily.

* * * *

At 10.30pm Mr Penby-Jones answered Doctor Penny's ring at the front door, having sent the House Maid to bed. The two men discussed Alice and the Doctor was thankfully told that she was certainly no worse and Nurse Wilmot was doing the night watch.

Very quietly the Doctor opened the bedroom-cum-sick room door and went in smiling at Nurse Wilmot. "How goes it?" he whispered. The nurse rose from her bedside chair and in true hospital fashion stood to attention in front of him. She reached for a special sheet that recorded all the necessary 'hourly' information about the little patient. She then quietly recited all she had noted since Doctor Penny had last seen Alice and he added his own notes in the space provided. "She has had a very good early evening and taken some broth and a drop of soda water." Nurse Wilmot smiled and held up crossed fingers.

"Good, but have there been many paroxysms?" said the Doctor.

"Not in the last hour Doctor" enthused the Nurse.

Doctor Penny made his usual thorough chest examination and was pleased with what he heard, yet seeing all this had started by his meeting – a pure chance meeting – with Alice and Nanny in the park some twelve hours before, he had to admit to never seeing whooping cough get worse – and improve so within the time period.

Doctor Penny had to brace himself for any sudden deterioration, so to help the cough and give Alice a truly good night's sleep he gave to Nurse Wilmot a packet of 'Dover's Powder grain 1/8th' should Alice become worse again in the night. "Nurse please don't hesitate to call me at any time should you think things are critical between now and morning." He then sat a while by the child's bed thinking.

* * * *

Mrs Prince the Doctor's housekeeper was – like her employer – an early riser. Spot on six each morning she took to his bedroom a large cup of strong tea, plus his shaving water. His retirement from practice had not changed his daily routine. After the tea and meticulous shave Doctor Penny would relax in his morning bath, after which he would dress; his clothes having been put out by the housemaid as instructed by Mrs Prince.

He had told Mr Penby-Jones that, unless called before, he would come to the house between eight-thirty and nine o'clock, a wise hour to observe the morning condition of Alice. A weakness the Doctor would not openly admit was that he always had a sinking feeling when he rang the bell on such a serious visit. The door was opened by the Penby-Jones' housemaid. She smiled broadly and giving him a 'bob' she blurted out "Little Miss Alice is ever so much better this morning!"

The Doctor smiled too. "I'm so pleased to hear it Jenny." He never forgot a name. Yet he was surprised as well as pleased.

A very tired looking Nurse Wilmot stood looking down at Alice who seemed much brighter, but still not out of the 'infectious wood'. "You look worn out Nurse. Have you had any sleep at all?" The Doctor looked about him. "And where is Nurse Watkins?" Nurse Wilmot was in the process of taking Alice's morning temperature. She looked at the reading in the thermometer and returned it to the little jar of antiseptic and water. She wrote the reading on the chart, then turned to Doctor Penny. "I'm sorry Doctor Penny. Nanny Watkins is lying down with a headache. She has felt unwell most of the night. "

"You have held the fort all night Nurse Wilmot?" asked the Doctor.

"I suppose I must have" came a professional reply, "but it was worth it. Alice is much improved. Her temperature is down and the whooping and coughing is much less." Doctor Penny wondered just how much of this was due to the good old 'Dover's powders'. Again he went over the infant lungs and heart, and was both satisfied and a bit astounded. "Let us have a chat in your room Nurse" he smiled.

* * * *

A small 'toy room' off Alice's bedroom had been converted – only yesterday – for Nurse Wilmot. (Nanny retained her own quarters where she slept for the moment.) Nurse Wilmot sat the

Doctor down in a comfortable chair and briefly left to make them both a strong cup of tea. While this was in progress Dr Penny made a rough calculation in his 'day book' as to the progress of the illness. It was far too rapid. Something was wrong, yet it could not be anything other than whooping cough.

When Nurse returned with the tea and she too settled down with a sigh, Doctor Penny began to review the case.

"Nurse, I would not normally suggest this, but you are a very well qualified fever Nurse and have had much experience of children I understand." Nurse Wilmot seemed to quickly understand his questioning. "Yes Doctor of course. There is nothing amiss I trust?"

"No, but well you see there is a strange aspect of this case. The aspect of the time factor." He opened his Day Book again. "As you have doubtless heard I came upon Alice by chance in the park. I thought she looked unwell and perhaps had a cold. Nanny Watkins claimed she had been quite well, but Alice gave a cough that, while then not truly 'pertussis' in character could not be ignored. Hence my swift action in sending her home and making a first visit within the hour. I have to say I instantly became sure the child had been symptomatic for a while. These had for some reason been overlooked."

Nurse Wilmot looked shocked. "That implies that Nanny was at best unobservant or at worst...well careless. I should perhaps tell you that in the short time I have been here I have got on well with her, but she has seemed apprehensive of tending to Alice – scared almost. Or scared of the possible prognosis in one so young. How sad for a Nurse."

They finished their tea and returned to look at the sleeping Alice. They found her sitting up in bed; even singing a little song to herself. She smiled at them. Though weak she said "I think I feel not so poorly now."

"Then it is time you had a special visitor" said Doctor Penny. "Nurse Wilmot, please ask Mr Teddy to come back to his bed."

"Certainly Doctor. He has had his medicine and would love to be back with Alice." As Nurse fetched the beloved teddy, Doctor Penny told Alice she was on the mend. Then he asked "How long have you felt poorly my dear? In my book it's only two days." Alice shook her head and told him that she had said to Nanny 'lots of days ago' she had a snuffle and a cough.

* * * *

It was time to have a look at Nanny Watkins. Nurse Wilmot took Doctor Penny to the Nanny's quarters on the floor above. Nanny was awake and agreed to let the old man check her over. She appeared anxious and drawn and the Doctor thought she might have been weeping. "Do you feel very ill Miss Watkins?" he asked, at the same time feeling her pulse. He knew he would have to tread carefully.

"I fear Doctor that I am actually a very anxious person, in truth not really cut out to be a Nurse." Tears rolled down her drawn face.

"Where did you do your training Miss Watkins? Was it locally or are you a London girl?" His voice was gentle yet she knew he wanted to get to the bottom of her background.

"I did train in London. At the Royal Free"

"A good place" Doctor Penny concurred. "Then I suppose you did the paediatric nursing course?"

"Yes. At Great Ormond Street. But you see I failed to get the qualification. I failed the certificate twice. I was gently eased out, but one could put it that way. Matron suggested I either went back to adult nursing or, as I loved children became a Nanny. So here I am."

"But I cannot quite see why you are so anxious my dear" the Doctor asked. Nanny Watkins then blurted out the whole sorry tale. It was one not unknown to him and had been traumatic for her. She had made the fatal mistake of getting too close to a child – a child with a fever whom she had nursed day and night, sadly to no avail. The illness was 'pertussis' – whooping cough just as Alice had it. But there was a great difference. She had spotted it early, but unlike Doctor Penny, a lazy doctor had not been astute enough in his diagnosis. His belief was, children are far more resilient than doctors and nurses give them credit for, and most coughs and sneezes come to nothing! Nurse had pleaded with him to come to the ward. He just told her to 'up the dose of Belladonna' the child was on and he would see her on the morning round. The child died half an hour before it started!

Apparently the doctor had told Ward Sister that Nurse Watkins could not have followed his advice. Sister referred the matter to Matron, and after that Nurse Watkins was told that 'doctor's words and advice were sacrosanct and must never-but-never be questioned!'

Nurse Watkins was mortified, and after a long stay in the Lake District with her sister took a Nanny course in Nottingham and some leisure work at the Children's Hospital to regain her nerve. She also re-sat her 'paediatric certificate' and passed.

She had been with the Penby-Jones's a year, but had not enjoyed good health, the 'nerves' returning around Christmas time. Alice had several coughs and colds, so Nanny fell back on the silly advice of a young House Officer with little real experience of paediatrics. Now with a true case of the dire 'pertussis' revealed, Nanny Watkins was ready to leave all things medical forever. Thus during the last night she had left Nurse Wilmot to care for Alice at a critical phase of her whooping cough. She did not hear of the improvement in the night, nor admit to observing symptoms many days before.

"Well here's a 'how-do-you-do' "said Dr Penny. "You may be surprised but I think we will be losing a good Nurse, and all because of a false premise spoken by a fool!"

Doctor Penny suggested he give Nanny Watkins a mild sedative from his bag. She agreed to a three-grain 'Bromural' tablet to calm her after her long confession. The Doctor said he would explain her illness in a way that would not make anyone think she was a neurotic. A vague reference to some family problem – an illness perhaps that might necessitate a short break when Alice was better. He always looked on the positive side. Nurse Watkins agreed fully with him, then slipped into a blissful repose.

* * * *

Back with Nurse Wilmot and a further improved Alice, Doctor Penny made a thorough examination just to make sure. The fever was all but gone. The cough had only the slightest of 'whoops' and the vomiting reduced to a weak retch. Now they must concentrate on a recovery period followed by a good convalescence, perhaps abroad. It was time to have a frank chat with the Penby-Joneses. Mr Penby-Jones had taken time off from his lace business until the crisis was reached and over…be it happy or very sad.

The Doctor's expression told all as he entered the morning room. "You look as if the news is good Doctor Penny. Is that so?" asked an eager Mrs Penby-Jones. "You are hopeful Doctor?" Mr Penby-Jones, a weak smile on his face, sought comfort.

"I am very hopeful, but will feel even more so if Alice has no relapse in the next forty-eight hours and gets stronger by the day."

He then carried on to clarify the current situation and touch on Alice's treatment and suggested help with her return to full health. The question he as dreading was why the illness had been so short. Mrs Penby-Jones had had experience of it he recalled, albeit with a sad conclusion. Fortunately no such question was posed. They very sensibly concentrated on the positive outlook.

"Alice is getting well enough – and please do not expect her to be up and about for at least a fortnight. Rest is all-important due to the strain that may have been placed on her heart, yet I don't see real signs of this. It's just a precaution you understand." The Doctor was becoming more cheerful.

"I suppose then a period of convalescence would be advisable" Mrs Penby-Jones asked brightly. "Some time away perhaps?" Doctor Penny said that was just what he was thinking. Perhaps by the sea.

It transpired that the Penby-Jones family had a delightful country retreat at 'Rosemullion Head' way down in South West Cornwall close to the Helford River, and as soon as Doctor Penny felt Alice was well enough to travel, this would give her considerable sea and country air to dispel her illness. Then a dark cloud appeared on the family horizon. Nanny Watkins, as soon as she was up and about, tendered her resignation, and looked to 'scupper' the good plans.

* * * *

The first Doctor Penny heard of the domestic blow was after Nurse Wilmot was asked if she could stay a while longer, for in truth her 'Hospital loan time' was coming to its conclusion. Fortunately the 'pertussis' bug had not developed into an epidemic, although a few children had caught it. Thankfully and rarely there had been no deaths reported locally.

As usual the matron of the Children's Hospital and 'Fever Sister' were very willing to continue with their help.

One afternoon, having visited his 'only' patient these days, Doctor Penny spared the time to visit Matron and tell her how the case had gone and chat generally of the prognosis both medical and 'domestic'. Matron knew of the Nanny's rather odd departure!

"I hope the Penby-Jones' were given a good reason for the Nanny's sudden departure?" Matron asked Doctor.

"I seem to think they were not altogether surprised" said Doctor Penny. "Confidentially, I have the impression that Nanny, while a worthy, caring soul, was not altogether cut out for such work." He could be very discreet in such matters.

Doctor Penny swiftly, yet politely changed the subject, yet Matron had a surprise for him. "Doctor, did you know that Nurse Wilmot – one of my best girls I would add – has approached me on the matter of leaving a good Nursing career to become a Nanny. Alice Penby-Jones' Nanny!"

"Well, I have to admit that does not altogether surprise me." Matron raised her eyebrows at Doctor Penny's reply to her announcement. The Doctor continued "Alice has become rather fond of Nurse Wilmot; but I sympathise with you Matron. A good specialist Nurse is rather an asset, especially a fever nurse. A wearisome job often with an unhappy outcome. Dare I ask if you have given your reluctant blessing to such an arrangement?"

Matron smiled. "Nurse Wilmot is such a sweet girl I could do no other. But I have told her there will always be a job at this Children's Hospital for her should she ever need one. Little girls do grow up fast these days. And of course Nurse Wilmot may suddenly find a grand young man – a doctor perhaps – to 'Squire' her."

Doctor Penny burst out laughing. "Well I have to say sadly I am out of the frame so to speak!" Both of them agreed Nurse Wilmot would make someone a wonderful wife.

* * * *

Spring bloomed and in another two weeks Doctor Penny agreed that Alice – now so much better – and taking good light food and 'Virol' (for growing girls as the advertisements had it) could look forward to going down to the family retreat in Cornwall. He did however make the proviso that she should keep clear of other children, but it was an isolated spot. Nurse, now 'Nanny' Wilmot went to see the Doctor for last minute instructions a few days before the family left.

Alice was having her afternoon nap when Nanny Wilmot slipped out into the sunshine after a late lunch. Jenny, the Housemaid, promised to keep an eye on the child, should she wake before Nanny's return.

Standing on the worn step of the Surgery door at Doctor Penny's – she still did not feel she could use the front door – the well-rung bell echoed down a passage, to be answered by the Doctor himself. He was expecting her.

Taking Nanny Wilmot into his surgery they chatted away about the coming Cornish holiday. Nanny Wilmot had never until now ventured so far South West. She was a local girl from a good middle-class home but not one which had been able to take such summer breaks; her father having to holiday at his Insurance firm's dictates, and then for but a week. She was surprised when Doctor Penny admitted that he too had in the past taken only short breaks, due to the business of finding and teaching suitable 'locum' doctors, not all of whom were ever truly satisfactory in his eyes. Nor had he ever been to Cornwall.

The small talk over they got down to the matter of Nanny's care of Alice while away.

"I will provide you with some more medicine to give general relief should Alice have a relapse, which is doubtful. Also a box of our old friend 'Dovers Powders' are worth having. However do enquire, when you arrive, who is the nearest doctor. I will give you a general letter to acquaint him with the case should you need him."

"You are so kind dear Doctor Penny" Nurse Wilmot remarked. She continued "You even care for us from a distance while we are away on holiday. I will of course take my nursing bag, fully stocked and to which I will add what you see fit to give me." For a moment the Doctor thought to himself "Here is a truly good

Nurse." "The maxim always have a bag to hand applies equally to nurses and doctors my dear!"

With a sincere promise to drop him a regular line with a progress report, Nanny Wilmot took Doctor Penny's hand. It was a brief but affectionate moment, and he hoped that his fatherly affection for her was not too obvious. Little did he know a similar feeling was mutual – Nanny Wilmot actually having lost her own father many years ago "I would both greatly appreciate and enjoy hearing from you Miss Wilmot" he smiled. He paused then continued "By the way, I wondered if you have heard any word from Miss Watkins since she left so unexpectedly. I wish I could have done more to make her stay."

Nurse Wilmot's pretty face clouded over. She looked shocked. "Obviously you have not spoken with Mrs Penby-Jones about Nanny Watkins."

"No, not for many days. She has always been out when I called. Is there something seriously amiss? I can 'read' faces you know."

Nanny Wilmot's eyes filled with tears. "Miss Watkins is dead" she stammered out. "It is so sad. She took her own life while staying in the Lake District."

The Doctor looked shocked. "I am deeply sorry to hear that. I will telephone Mrs Penby-Jones this evening. Would you kindly let her know." Nanny Wilmot said she would do so.

It was essential that Doctor Penny had to hand all the details he had on his consultation with Miss Watkins, for he felt he must speak with the Coroner in the case.

* * * *

Mrs Penby-Jones was traditionally 'vague' on the matter of Miss Watkins leaving and demise. It had all been very inconvenient for the family, but they were grateful when the hospital had allowed Miss Wilmot (such a nice girl) to resign her post and come over to them. Miss Watkins had been satisfactory but never as good as the original and beloved Nanny Grayling – sadly too old to come back.

A word with Doctor Liddle, the local Coroner, soon produced the name and address of the Coroner dealing with the deceased Miss Watkins up in the Lake District. She had been staying near Lake Windermere. A solicitor – Major Pears – who worked out of Kendal had a wide jurisdiction.

Doctor Penny put a trunk call through to the Solicitor's office. Very fortunately Major Pears was in, and very glad to speak to a doctor who had so recently had some dealings with the deceased party. An inquest had not yet taken place, there being so little background information to hand. Death was clearly a suicide, Miss Watkins having taken a large dose of the barbiturate 'Veronal'. She had left a note merely indicating she intended to die by her own hand.

From the notes in his 'day book' the Doctor related his brief professional contact with the deceased. He briefly told the story of how he had come across Alice Penby-Jones – his former patient - and spotted possible pertussis, yet Nanny Watkins was rather dismissive of his advice. He 'cut to the chase' and told of his misgivings with regard to Nanny and how he had got a specialist paediatric fever nurse in to help out. He then found Nanny had taken to her bed. She had no discernable illness, but he felt she was perhaps an undiagnosed depressive. He had given her a grain 3 tablet of the sedative 'Bromural' to settle her and did advise her to see her usual practitioner when up and about. This was the last he saw of her, for the next day she left the household.

Major Pears thanked him and asked the leading question – did Doctor Penny think the deceased had been already on barbiturates? He thought not. At least she denied the use of any hypnotic.

"How did the parents of your patient take Nanny Watkins' departure?"

"They were, I understand 'un-moved', but I think this was due to the fact that the Nurse I got in had offered to take her place if they were inclined to have her. For them the problem was solved, and that was that. Actually it was a fortunate move for the little girl liked the Nurse Wilmot very much."

Major Pears, the Kendal Coroner, expressed a wish to ring Mrs Penby-Jones in case she had any more information about relatives of the deceased. Doctor Penny had no objection but privately felt the Major would get precious little else out of the lady.

* * * *

And so the middle-class 'respectable' family went off on their Cornish holiday to benefit the recovery of Alice. April showers indeed brought the May flowers which followed on the usual early primroses which Nanny Wilmot and Alice picked for the house. They were a happy band, but it was not to last too long. On the 10th May King Edward VII died, throwing the whole country into mourning. It would mean a prompt return home as Mr Penby-Jones had to organise the expected events from his business – church services and such-like. So the family departed for home in sombre attire.

Sitting in his empty surgery Doctor Penny, similarly dressed, thought of the telegram in his hand sent by Nurse Wilmot to say the holiday had come to an end but Alice was so much better and they would call on him while on a walk in the park. The Doctor silently cursed the old rogue of a King. "I would think it was all those damn cigars!" he muttered!

1918 – Captain Rhodes and the Spanish Lady

The young R.A.M.C Captain peered intensely at his service wrist watch. It was a few minutes off eleven in the morning. It had also been made generally known that at the eleventh hour of the eleventh day of the eleventh month 1918 would see end to the most dreadful hostilities ever known. All over the theatre of war the horror would stop. Where Captain Rhodes was, at this precise time, the front went on for eighty odd miles. He really wondered if the 'general order to cease fire would be adhered to? There were some Americans who sought to go on to Germany and generally clean up. Yet on sober reflection Bill realized that all the fighting men of so many nations had gone through more than enough.

On the dot of eleven many guns stopped firing, bar the odd burst from an enthusiastic machine gunner. Men, both British and German, were still struggling in 'no mans land', and this claimed a few unlucky souls.

In many respects the 'Top Brass' managed to cock it up yet again, some screaming casualties needed help to remain alive until Bill and his stretcher bearers got through the Flanders mud to give them aid and get the wounded back to the nearest Regimental Aid post still viable in their trench.

Once back at the R.A.P these wounded who had 'got Blighty ones' were treated. They were lucky. A couple of their pals did not live to see the desired peace.

For some strange reason Bill tried to take in an overall perspective of his work as a military 'medic' here. Particularly so since the German spring offensive, which had lasted some four months, yet had floundered at the River Marne just outside Paris. This was largely due to the allied counter attack by the French and American forces during August 1918. Casualties had been – as usual – in this bloody awful war- heavy on all sides. And Bill had sweated for long hours as the most ghastly battle injuries came through his hands.

The trench in which he now splashed around had been held for a month by American troops. They were now suffering with the same triumvirate of mud, blood and trench feet. A basic curse for all medical personnel when anywhere in the landscape a shell had been fired to cause such surroundings. Men stood for days in mud and contaminated water, sometimes up to their waist. When overcome with tiredness they would fall and become submersed in his filthy hell.

In addition to trench feet, trench fever presented medical problems, a complication of neglected or prolonged trench foot would be gangrene, leading to amputation in the extreme instances. Trench fever could mimic any febrile illness, but influenza was often misdiagnosed and understandably so. This turned out to have serious consequences in the weeks following the excitement of the 'peace.'

An American doctor had very swiftly and efficiently sorted out the wounded from, hopefully, the last shell of the war in this sector. And he had taken an urgent message to ask Captain Rhodes, when he appeared, to make his way to talk to the sister at the Clearing Station further behind the line. The message was duly given as the American medic was dressing a minor hand wound caused by a fragment of shrapnel. A new 2nd. Lieut. Of the Notts and Derby Regiment ('The Sherwood Foresters') that had just come up the line to join in the final throws of the war. Dr Rhodes said he would see the young officer safely to the clearing Station, where they would decide what should happen next to this pleasant and stoic chap who had undoubtedly arrived at the right time, yet caught a 'Blighty one.'

* * * *

The excellent Sister Berridge collared Dr 'Bill' as soon as he stepped foot inside the doors of the Clearing station a safe distance behind the line. Sister was a person for whom he had great respect. He had never seen her 'flap' no matter how dire the circumstance, yet now she did have a worried look about her. He gave her one of his most charming smiles. "Sister, how good to see you on this wonderful day."

"Indeed it is Dr Rhodes, yet I fear we may have a serious problem blowing up for us and just as deadly as a 'Mills bomb', thrown in no-mans land!" She lowered her voice and murmured. "I am speaking of the dreaded enemy, influenza."

Bill replied quietly in kind. "Actually Sister, I did hear in the Officers' mess at H.Q. something about a Reuters's message via the line from Madrid, that the people there have suffered badly, and with a high mortality. As you know Sister we have had a few unexpected deaths among men whose wounds could not have proved fatal on their own. "Sister looked relieved that he had told her all this, for she had had her own experience of a 'flu type of late.

"Indeed Dr Rhodes. I have suddenly lost two nurses and a V.A.D girl in a similar way. An infection I took to have come via their patients during treatment. I asked to see you today to see how we might possibly contain things effectively?" Bill Rhodes thought for a moment. "Sister is that special holding ward in use at the moment?"

"No doctor, it is having what one might call a 'deep clean' after the last crowd of German P.O.W's stayed a night under guard in it, and we had sorted out the various degrees of injury. Oh my Lord!" She stopped looking horrified. Bill asked "Are you going to tell me that there were more fever cases among them?" "Yes indeed" said Sister. "I distinctly heard one man mumble something about 'le grippe' – to quote the French troops. These prisoners had originally been taken by the French, but they did not have enough men to march them through so ours were asked to take it on. You know how chaotic everything is.

Sister Berridge smiled and took Bill through to the Holding Ward located at the end of a long passage. The wonderful nursing staff and V.A.D girls had already cleaned every part of the large, airy ward with that most powerful of disinfectants 'Lysol', a saponified mixture of cresol and oil, soluble in water.

"Will this suffice?" Sister asked. "It will be for say thirty six beds at least, only the true influenza cases of course, yet while I hate to say it, many will be 'short term guests' if what I hear is true." And as they were alone in the ward Bill put his arm around her shoulders as he murmured what they both recognized was a wistful platitude.

By chance far less ill men arrived. A mixed bunch but amazingly cheerful – both friend and foe alike- indeed the odd general feeling that since the armistice, friend and foe did not exist. For Heaven's sake the bloody war was over!

Bill Rhodes did not speak German, but found that the Germans put most of the allied troops to shame by speaking very good English, which made his job much easier when examining those obviously with minor wounds or illnesses. Their ills were just the same as the other fellows round about. There was an Officer of the German Army present who had been with his men when they were held but twenty minutes before the allotted hour of 11am. Politely he drew Bill to one side and spoke of the febrile state of some of the men, even though he tried to smile through it. They too had lost a large number due to 'flu'.

Both officers had heavily stained and mud splattered uniforms, so it was only after a while conversing, did Bill realize that he was in the company of a German Medical Officer. He gave his apologies and hoped he had not caused offence in this 'very new' situation. Bill asked, although not knowing the other man's actual rank, "well my dear Sir if you can throw your English on the specific condition of you chaps; I see no reason why we should not 'do a round' together. The German medic smiled and replied, "Indeed my dear Dokter, if it is not against your rules I would be glad to come round with you. Some of the men are not too fluent in English and I am sure you will agree a good 'history' is essential to diagnosis and the right treatment."

Doctor Bill was impressed by his young counter-part who must have gone through much the same as he. They both realized they had not introduced themselves. Bill held out his hand. "I am Captain William Rhodes of our Royal Army Medical Corps. I am of course 'Bill' to my colleagues, or 'Dr Bill' to more junior ranks in private." The other man laughed. "And I, Dr Rhodes am Dr –

presently Captain – Manfred Sprengel. I have been in our medical Service for two years. I dare say we have endured similar dreadful events and stress." Of recent times Bill had treated the sick and wounded of both sides. The enemy on the face of it was polite and grateful for his and all the medical, nursing and ancillary staff care extended to them while as P.O.W patients. He was always surprised when some-one would say 'good lord they are nearly as human as ourselves!' Why should they not be so? It was the 'press' with their frenetic articles; largely exaggerated to make the Great British public hate the Hun to an even greater extent. Truth to tell in this Great War, now ended, each side had to obey orders like it or not. And quietly also on a personal note each felt at least a modicum of sympathy for the wounds of the opposite numbers.

As Bill Rhodes mused this point he hadn't heard Captain Sprengel excuse himself, as some more of his men had arrived. They were very ill.

A stretcher party led by Sister Berridge carried four men to the 'cots' duly allocated. Sister was trying to keep surgical and medical cases on opposite sides of the ward. The man nearest to Bill looked very near moribund. He was coughing up large amounts of yellow/green sputum; his sweaty face was 'heliotrope' in colour. Manfred Sprengel appeared at the soldier's side, speaking to him in German, whilst taking a stethoscope from his tunic pocket. Bill automatically followed suit.

Within thirty minutes the first German patient, turned his face to the wall and died. Bill Rhodes pronounced him dead, for technically Manfred Sprengel was not on the list of Medical Officers. By this time three other men – all German – fell ill in the same manner and with the same ghastly speed. Even sister Berrridge was horribly alarmed, but found more orderlies and V.A.D's to help with the wildfire of malaise. Bill and Manfred agreed it was the spread of so called Spanish 'Flu' or 'the Spanish Lady'.

There followed urgent, yet secret contact with the top Medical Brass at H.Q. Captain Rhodes put in a request for extra doctors and orderlies, while sister Berridge consulted with her Nursing Officers. If anything she knew she would need far more nurses and V.A.D's. for both medical and nursing staff official advice was needed with regards to the best line of management for troops coming in with any hint of influenza.

Amazingly for the Army a quick decision was made in their favour, and to Bill Rhodes' pleasure Captain Manfred Sprengel was allowed by his superiors to stay put as it was clear that more captured Germans were coming through that sector. He was clearly a respected Officer and a great help to the Clearing Station.

Bill Rhodes put in an urgent order for more drugs of a more simple kind, such as ammoniated tincture of quinine and the old standby 'Dovers Powders', both excellent anti pyretics in the initial stages of the illness, but this flu' was obviously more virulent and rapid.

Several more men went down with the early signs and symptoms of influenza. Fever, sore throat and a 'barking' cough that became very productive of mucopurelant sputum. All were isolated as far as possible. Also there were still casualties with recent wounds, or post-operative wounds to dress. And a few still died, in some cases a merciful relief. And then the flu' swept through the hospital, laying low patients and staff alike. Some seemed better for a while, then suddenly worsened and died.

At least all the remaining soldiers had been treated until well enough to be taken to a more extensive hospital nearer to the coast, and duly returned to home. As for the German P.O.W troops they were handed over to their own medical staff and whatever arrangements were in place for them. For a very tired Captain Rhodes the time soon came to say goodbye to Captain Manfred Sprengel. Bill gave Manfred his home address and hoped that they would keep in touch, for they had been through a 'short hell' together. A happy result of the 'Peace'.

* * * *

Towards the end of November 1918, just as Bill Rhodes was getting his own things together for the move to H.Q and hopefully the 'light of demobilisation' when a letter in his sister's hand reached him via the usual convoluted way. His mother was none too well with what was considered to be an attack of bronchitis. This was not something new to her and the family doctor's usual medicine seemed to be 'doing the trick', so Emma wrote. The date of posting was a fortnight previously.

Bill Rhodes was naturally very anxious, for he had heard talk in the Officer's mess of how rife this so called Spanish influenza was back home in England, with London full of cases. The army medics were even admitting that they were better off with a known number of possible patients, rather than the poor old general practitioners in 'town' (meaning London). Few had seen the obituary columns, day after day. Bill wrote a positive letter home, and did get it past the Official Censor to be marked URGENT by the Army Postal Service. By good chance he also had more post from home which would cross with his letter. Mother was still at home, yet not really any better.

Old Dr Briggs was gently asking if there would be any chance of Bill getting some compassionate leave? It would mean a medical man in the home and old Mrs Rhodes could have expert attention to herself. Dr Briggs would still call last thing at night.

Bill knew that this request would not be even considered without much thought. He was very fond of the old G.P who had in years past helped him with his medical studies as a student at the London Hospital.

The Staff Officers at H.Q. did not in any way try to prevent Captain Rhodes – who for Heaven's sake had the M.C & Bar, for his brave work tending casualties in the 'field' and back at two Regimental Aid Posts; he was responsible for in his time at the front. No, Captain Rhodes must be dispatched home forthwith on the next boat train. Quietly all hoped he would be able to find his mother better and on the mend.

* * * *

Every Army Officer was used to packing up and setting off to any destination on the signing of a 'chitty', so Bill Rhodes was whisked to Dover and on a Hospital Train to London. The connecting train from Dover sped on to London, with no stops to hold it up. For this Bill was glad as in truth he was beginning to feel unwell. His throat was very sore and his brow pouring with sweat. He guessed he had a raging temperature. When an orderly offered him a mug of tea he accepted and took from his pocket a bottle of 'Tabs. Dover'. A couple of these should get him home. He took them using a swig from his silver hip flask which held a decent amount of 'Black and White' whiskey (Officers for the use of!) On reflection perhaps a soporific concoction, but badly needed.

In the taxi from the Station he began to feel a bit better; at least his throat was duly numbed. And at last he was at the front gate of home. Amazingly Dr Briggs was opening it and on his way out. He looked exhausted. Dr Briggs paused as Bill paid off the taxi, whose driver gave a great sneeze, minus a handkerchief. Both Doctors looked at each other in dismay. Dr Briggs began their conversation. "You mother is a real fighter, Bill. I am afraid that a patch of basal lobe pneumonia seems to be present in her right lung. I would suggest a spell in hospital, but so many medical wards are packed with folk with chest complications from this 'bloody' 'flu'. Fortunately her temperature has gone down and she is getting rid of a lot of infected phlegm as far as I can make out."

The elderly doctor peered at Bill Rhodes, saying "if you don't mind my professional observation, you look far from bright yourself. Starting flu' do you think?"

"I well could be Doctor. But I am pretty well immune to everything going, having spent many hours in dug-outs half full of mud, filthy water, blood and dead rats."

"Is there any flu' over there?" Dr Briggs asked, adding "You do realise that we were only told what the politicians want us to know back home."

"Well if the daft buggers don't think France and indeed what up until the 11th hour etc. was fighting hell cannot be part of the flu' pandemic they are more gormless than we in the thick of it took them for!"

By now Emma had run to the gate and threw her arms around her brother. Dr Briggs decided he must get on with his visits.

* * * *

Bill was pleased to at least see his sister was looking well. She must have nursed mother day and night, yet by good chance did not catch the flu' from so doing, but now she would be very exhausted and run down. She took Bill up to see mother. The old lady was asleep. She sighed and opened her eye. "Is that you my Billy boy?"

"How are you feeling 'Mater?' You have had a blast of the old bronchitis I hear."

The old lady tried to raise from her pillows and went into a paroxsysm of coughing. Bill went into automatic 'doctor mode'. "Easy now mum. Where is the medicine Dr Briggs has given you?" She pointed to a side table with bottles and other nursing items upon it. Looking through these Bill noted that Dr Briggs had already started his patient on a low dose of digitalis to combat any heart failure. He would have liked to 'sound' mother's chest but he knew that without Dr Briggs being present with him at the time this would have been medically impolite; even a shade unethical. He did observe her pattern of breathing and her colour. She was not nearly out of the woods yet. And he was rather conscious of his own condition. The 'Tabs. Dover' and the whiskey were wearing off. He went into the room Emma had got ready for him and rummaged in his portmanteaux for the few instruments he had brought home with him. He took a clinical thermometer in his spirit proof tubular case out and after washing it, placed the mercury bulb under his filthy tongue. It read 104 degrees Celsius. Neither was he out of the woods. Then he found his stethoscope and attempted to listen to his chest sounds. Always a futile clinical check on oneself. Yet he could make out a fast heartbeat. Bill thought perhaps a breath of fresh air, and a pipe of tobacco in the garden might help. First another swig from the flask.

He sat on the garden seat and felt like death 'warmed up'. Then the back gate opened. Through sore and aching eyes Bill saw the caller was his lovely Mary. Mary Travelyon was a librarian and an old school friend of Emma. She and Bill had what was politely referred to 'an understanding' – the preliminary to engagement. It had been a long drawn out matter, on hold until the war had ended and Bill had decided what branch of medicine in which he would settle.

Now Mary slowly walked towards him, a shade tongue- tied for she had not seen Bill for nearly a year. And there hadn't been any time to send a letter when he knew he was bound for home.

When Mary approached, Bill gestured that she should not attempt to embrace him. She had guessed from his drawn face, so flushed and perspiring he was ill, doubtless with the awful flu' so prevalent. Several on her road had been struck down, and two had died within hours.

"Bill my love you of all should know bed is where you should be resting." He shook his head and in a husky voice told her he had just arrived home to see his Mother, but had fallen unwell during the journey. Just at that moment Emma ran into the garden to say Mother had shown difficulty in breathing, her face turning a deep purple. She had also turned to the wall.

Bill went upstairs as fast as he could make it. He needed no stethoscope to tell him she was dead. The influenza had struck again on top of her chest problems to which she had succumbed. And he felt it was his fault. In coming home he had become the Grim Reaper visiting his own family.

A short while later Dr Briggs returned, having received a message from Bill. The old boy was visibly upset having known his patient for many years. He was also so sad for Bill and Emma. And he was greatly concerned for Bill, saying he must know that bed was the right place for him. Out of Emma's hearing Bill told his old friend of the many influenza cases he had so recently seen at the field hospital and his own symptoms on the journey over from France. Dr Briggs drew him to one side and made the all too familiar examination. Bill told him what he had taken already. Dr Briggs took from his bag a small bottle from a box of several he had already prepared. "I'm afraid" he said "you will have guessed that this is tincture of Digitalis with Nux Vomica and spirits of ammonia."

"Then the heart is failing on top of the infection?"

"Not too bad at the moment. You know the doses. Take the lowest to begin with, 6 hourly."

At first Bill went and sat with his now peaceful Mother, gently holding a cold hand. Emma had been down to the undertaker whose premises were only in the next road. Fortunately they could 'do' for dear Mrs Rhodes, saying that two members of their staff would be at the house within the hour.

On Emma's return she found Bill trying to get into his bed. He was sweating and delirious. As she covered him with blankets he kept going on about another convoy of ambulances coming up from the front and to ask Sister to get the surgical team together. He began speaking to her as if she was a Nurse. Barking orders. Asking for instruments she had never heard of. Then with great fortune Dr Briggs walked in again. He had brought Mrs Rhodes's death certificate.

Emma realized that Dr Briggs had been working away without rest for days on end. Now he helped her with her stricken brother. He even helped sponge Bill down with tepid water, after which he gave an injection to relax if not totally sedate him. A larger bottle of medicine was taken from a small supply in his copious Gladstone bag. He explained how ill Bill was; gave nursing instructions and times for the medicine. He agreed to a brief rest with a cup of tea in the kitchen, but then made off on his old bicycle to another patient on his list of visits.

About midnight Bill Rhodes suddenly gasped and rapidly slipped into unconsciousness taking on the horrible 'heliotrope' colour. By 1am he was dead. Emma did all the usual things necessary, covered the body; went downstairs and wept. She was totally alone

* * * *

When after what seemed like an eternity the sky lightened with the dawn so Emma washed, dressed and had another strong cup of tea. Mother's funeral was arranged for two days hence due to the pressure on the undertakers, but she had to go down again to tell them about her brother's death.

The undertakers were very kind and indeed upset to hear of Dr Rhodes sudden passing, but this influenza pandemic was sweeping through the land, bringing death to so many homes. It was well-known that it had begun in Spain and was aptly called the 'Spanish lady'. If 'she called' it was said – with good cause- that someone in the family who break-fasted with them, might very well 'dine with their ancestors'.

Later in the morning, after Emma had returned from her sad funeral arranging, she found a tearful Mary sitting in the garden. A neighbour had told her of 'the dear Captain's death, following his mother so soon.' In the stoic British tradition yet another pot of tea was made and the two girls tried to keep up each other's Sprits. When the covered hearse came for Bill they returned to the parlour.

For two hours the friends talked about how much Bill had done in his time as a Battalion Medical Officer, tending what must have been horrific injuries in equally horrific conditions. On his brief spells of leave in three years he had said hardly anything about what he had faced in the trenches and his Regimental Aid Post.

Emma had heard other soldiers' wives say their loved ones never spoke of the travails they had to face. In fact when Bill had won his military cross in 1917 he merely said he had crawled to an officer lying injured in no-man's land, tended to his wounds and gave him some morphine before dragging him back through a hole in the wire. (He had said nothing of the shelling going on at the time.) Equally nothing had been mentioned of what he did to be honoured a second time. Emma also went to see the local Parish priest to discuss the services for both Mother and Brother Bill. When she got home she found letters from Bill's Senior Officer. A Nursing Sister who admired him had also written most kindly. Yet most surprisingly a letter with a German stamp. It was from a German Medical Officer named Manfred Sprengel, who had worked briefly with Bill after the Armistice. The doctor had been told of Bill's illness and death by Sister Berridge. He was charming in his condolences. Emma sorted all the letters in respect of Mother and Bill for due reply.

Due to the volume of work for all undertakers at this time in 1918, Mrs Rhodes and Bill her dear son, were interred together in a family grave at Kensal Green Cemetery, some ten days later. Emma Rhodes and her friend Mary Travelyon wept in genuine grief. Surprisingly there were a fair number of mourners, despite National advice for not too many persons to attend funerals, should they spread or catch the virulent illness from the 'Spanish Lady'.

The traditional funeral tea, 'with ham' was ready for those good folk who had attended to remember Bill Rhodes and his Mother both so well liked and respected, for it had been a very sad set of circumstances. Maybe Bill should not have come over to visit his mother, especially when he fully realized he was showing all the signs and symptoms of the Spanish influenza. He was glad however that she had seen him. Whether he had really contributed to her final demise was – as Dr Briggs had assured him was purely academic. In any event Bill had dealt with God knows how many cases before leaving France. He had been fine until the journey home. Sooner die at home than in a ghastly Clearing Station behind the supposedly silent lines.

'The Spanish lady' killed eight million in Spain alone, then millions throughout the world. It lessened, and then came back in

1919. The very young had suffered and died most often, and for reasons not fully known to the doctors young pregnant women were very likely to succumb. If there was any surviving issue of the union they joined the band of civilian orphans all over the world. The flu' actually killed more than did the slaughter of the Great War.

In the early 1920's two young ladies Emma Rhodes and Mary Travelyon who now lived together, such was their bond through the death of a man they both loved in separate ways, was with hard work and against so many odds, made in reality a fitting memorial.

* * * *

POSTSCRIPT

Emma Rhodes:

Emma Rhodes was left very well off financially by both her mother and Brother. She did not however rest in her new circumstances. She was very much aware that following the war and the influenza pandemic, there was a terrible shortage of both nurses and especially medical students. She decided on nursing, for in 1918 the London medical schools still did not accept female students, although things were soon to change.

An old friend offered help. Dr Briggs had survived the decimation of the flu', although in parts it was still taking its toll. Yet the old Doctor soldiered on and one day passing the Rhodes home popped in to see how Emma was managing. In conversation she expressed her wish to become a nurse and as the doctor was a luminary of St. Thomas's, with its fine School of nursing he offered to ring the Matron and Sister Tutor, prior to taking Emma along for an interview.

Emma Rhodes met with all the requirements and was offered a place at the start of the next academic term.

Never did she find out that at one time- long ago – Dr Briggs had been engaged to Matron!

Mary Travelyon:

Emma's old friend Mary had also survived the flu', but was still grieving for Bill. It seemed to her, as indeed with so many others that having given so much of himself tending to the severely wounded then dying of influenza just after the war had ended, was the act of a very unfair God. Mary refused to go to church for months after Bill's death.

An idea was building in her mind. Bill had also often commented that no women could undertake a medical course which allowed them access to any teaching hospital for the purpose of learning 'clinical medicine', nor could they learn anatomy by dissection of the human body in the same class as male students. But in 1869 three young ladies, Miss Sophia Jex Blake, Miss Mary Peachey and Miss Isobel Thorne requested permission to be admitted as perpetual pupils at St. Mary's Medical School. While back then this request was declined, it was clear that not all the teaching staff were against it, but of course then no women had been added to the Medical Register.

In 1874 Miss Jex Blake acquired a house and had if fitted out as a suitable place where women who wished to study medicine could enjoy every facility required. In addition a proper Council was formed to administer the 'school' to be officially named 'The London School for Medical Women'. Twenty- one members of the Council were from St. Mary's, one of whom acted as Dean.

* * * *

Great changes had taken place by the end of the Great War. And in the February of 1920 – in the same month as Dr Charles Wilson was appointed sub-Dean of St. Mary's Medical School – later to be given the title 'the Great Dean' – a female student of great promise, Mary Travelyon, stepped foot inside the Medical

School buildings in and around Norfolk Place, off Praed Street, Paddington.

Mary qualified in 1925 with the Conjoint Diploma – Member of the Royal College of Surgeons (Eng.) & Licentiate of the Royal College of Physicians (London). After several in house posts at her teaching hospital, she went on to specialize in Obstetrics at Queen Charlotte's famous hospital in the old Manor house, Lisson Green, where it had been since 1813.

Emma Rhodes became a fine Staff Nurse at St. Thomas's and rose to the post of 'Sister Casualty'.

All-in-all Bill Rhodes's bequests had been well used.

1920 – Her Last Penny

Even before the young cockerel had first crowed, Nancy was out in the golden morning mist, feeding the hens. On this glorious summer day – this most exciting day – she could not remain in her bed past five o'clock.

Mother watched from the cottage bedroom window and smiled to herself, understanding her little daughter's enthusiasm to be up and about. She too remembered school trips to the sea-side when she was a little girl back in the 1880s. And now the annual treat of 1920 was just as important to the village children, many of whom would otherwise never see the sea.

This year they were off to one of the smaller resorts on the Lincolnshire coast. Buckets and spades had been ready for days. Dreams of the pleasures of the beach had occupied both sleeping and waking hours.

Nancy looked up, smiled and waved madly through the mist at her mother. Mother waved back to that diminutive, tousled haired, skinny figure, brown as a berry. Nancy was her only child and especially close to her since the death of her husband and father in the influenza epidemic in 1918. Nancy had been brave and supportive despite her young years. A loving, giving child without a hint of malice in her nature. If anyone deserved a good treat it was little Nancy.

An important facet of the trip was the food for the great day. This came in the form of contributions of all sorts from family and friends of the school children. It would all be collected and placed in two large hampers. Nancy's mother had scrimped and saved to send her girl with something enjoyable. There were boiled egg sandwiches, and fish-paste sandwiches with mustard and cress, plus plum bread and a bottle of homemade ginger beer. All were freshly prepared within an hour of Nancy leaving for the school and the assembly of trippers.

As mother gave Nancy this packed lunch, she turned to the mantelshelf and opening a tin, took out six bright pennies, giving them to the child. It was not much, but six pennies would pay for a donkey ride, a couple of ice-creams and maybe a stick of rock. Nancy's eyes grew wide at the sight of the spending money. A lovely picnic and pennies in her dress pocket. What could go wrong with the day? She threw her arms around her mother's neck and gave her a big hug and a kiss.

They set off for the village school at 8 o'clock. Already a crowd had gathered – excited children with their parents and relatives. And drawn up outside the school gate were three huge farm wagons pulled by pairs of beautifully groomed shire horses, their coats and brasses gleaming, their manes be-ribboned. The wagons too were freshly painted – orange and blue, and adorned with streams of bunting.

Taking her lunch offering, Nancy handed it to the teacher to be packed into the hampers with all the other good things. The picnic being a communal affair, no-one knew whose offering they were eating, thus there were no jibes at those who could not, through force of circumstance, bring much. Not that anyone minded, with all the thrill of the day.

Kissing mother goodbye Nancy joined her friends. Mother walked away to the end of the village street to be ready to wave. Although they were only off for the day, she hated farewells.

At last the procession set off for the station. The cheers were deafening. As the second wagon passed, Mother could see Nancy's wide grin and furious waving as the horses clopped by. Was there perhaps a hint of nervousness in that smile? Was it a shade too jovial? Mother remembered how she had always had butterflies in the tummy on these occasions, and guessed Nancy had too. The seaside seemed so far away.

So the vibrant procession passed on to the railway station to board the patiently steaming train.

Excitement grew as the children scrambled out of the wagons and, in good order, passed on to the steamy platform. The very smell of the waiting train increased the thrill of things. With amazing efficiency the teachers and helpers got every child aboard and settled on the train – a seething mass of wriggling bodies in their summer best, clutching buckets and spades, and shrimping nets and towels in which were wrapped their bathing costumes. Then with a wave of the guard's flag and a toot from the engine, they were off.

It would not be a long journey yet for those who hinted at feeling sick, one of the teachers had lumps of barley sugar that seemed to quell the churning tummy. In case of real travel sickness one teacher had acquired from the village doctor a small number of hyoscine hydrobromide tablets; safe and effective.

Every minute of the journey was eagerly savoured by the children. Sights from the carriage windows were new and very exciting. For the last half mile or so, as the train rolled towards the sea-side station, the line ran along the coast with views of beaches, sand-dunes and in the distance the shimmering sea. All the children crowded over to that side of the train and cheered.

For those children who had not been on the trip before, this was their first sight of the North Sea. The whole scenario was to them magical; eyes were wide and hearts beating fast. This was Nancy's second trip, but still she enthused at the sunlight playing on the waves and the breeze blowing through the tall grasses of the dunes. If this was only the start, what joys were still to come?

The station marked the end of the line. Children and teachers spilled out on to the platform to the smell of sea, smoke and engine steam. Exciting smells of holidays.

After a quick roll call and the safe transferral of the precious lunch hampers to the trolley belonging to one of the local boys making a bob or two for transporting items of luggage to hotels and boarding houses – these would of course go to a point on the beach – the school trippers were moved into a 'crocodile' ready for their march to the sands.

Nancy sat gazing at the sea for what seemed an age. It was to her young eyes the most wonderful of sights – breakers showing their white crests far towards the horizon. The tide was now far out and there were along that flat golden beach occasional dips and pools of sea water embellished with that lovely seaweed that one could make 'pop'. Here was fun ready for the taking.

A little boy came and sat himself down next to Nancy. Tommy Palmer, son of the local mole catcher; a solitary child with no real friends. Nancy did not dislike him, but knew him to be a little moody and withdrawn. Looking at Tommy she saw on his face an expression of total awe and amazement. This was his first trip to the seaside. They said nothing, just sat there together taking it all in. While some might not think so, to them it was the most beautiful landscape. Then, when some of Nancy's friends called her to join them for a game of quoits, Tommy suddenly grabbed her arm and begged "Don't leave me!" There was fear on his little pinched face. Fear of the vast beach and the noisy sea ahead of him.

Although she hardly knew him, Nancy felt it would be hurtful to abandon Tommy with his fear to the great unknown of the seaside. So Tommy for once joined in the fun, whereas at school he would have been ignored. Still they didn't have much to say to one another, yet without a great deal of outward show Nancy took charge of Tommy; took him to see the Punch and Judy man; took him to find shrimps and minute crabs in the pools; showed him how to build a sand castle, even sharing her old wooden spade, for Tommy Palmer had brought no bucket and spade of his own. No one even knew if he had contributed any lunch, yet he looked eager and hungry when at last the children were organised around the food hampers and lunch was served.

When Nancy asked Tommy Palmer what he would like to eat, he simply said "anyfink". His eyes were as wide at the sight of the food as they had been at the sight of the sea. When Nancy told the teacher that she was going to take a plate of sandwiches and a drink of ginger beer for Tommy, she looked over to the forlorn little figure on the edge of the group and whispered gently "Be extra nice to him Nancy. This is his first time out of the village, and it is all very strange for him. A bit frightening too I would imagine."

Nancy understood very well. She too had felt the loneliness of the outcast on occasions. She felt in her pocket to reassure herself that the special pennies were safe.

So they sat and ate a sandwich lunch. Sand in the sandwiches, and in the ginger beer, but that only added to the enjoyment! This was the most exciting thing they had done so far this year, as exciting as Christmas Eve. They were two happy 'waifs' from a Lincolnshire village.

"Wish my mum was here" said Tommy! "She could see the sea too. She had never seen the sea." Hearing this, Nancy began to feel extra sad for Tommy, and his mum. Never to have seen the sea. It was something everyone should do. It was living! Then she suggested they collect some shells and pebbles for him to take home to his mum. She could at least listen to the roar of the sea in a shell if she put it to her ear. Tommy liked the idea.

Persuading the boys to let Tommy join in a game of beach cricket, Nancy left him for a moment to take some time to herself. She walked awhile, not too far from the group, and came across a little stall selling sticks of rock with the name of the resort written through the centre. With one of her pennies she bought a pink, stripey stick for her mother. Then after much inward debate, with two more pennies bought for herself a little rag doll in very bright clothes. It would be a memento of this happy day. Something tangible to keep for ever.

Several of her friends now joined her, and they, together with a teacher decided to go for a donkey ride. After this fun Nancy surveyed her spending money. There were now only two pennies left. She considered if she spent just one more on an ice-cream, and saved the remaining one, then mother would be pleased with her thoughtfulness. Spend some, save some. This was the motto in their home. It was a way of remaining happy.

Nancy had only just turned round from the 'stop-me-and-buy-one' man's tricycle when she found Tommy Palmer beside her again. He said nothing but looked longingly at Nancy's ice-cream cornet. It was obvious that poor Tommy had no spending money of his own, so Nancy, with a surge of compassion, gave him her last penny, saying to buy himself a cornet too. Her mother would understand. She always said it was good to do a kindness for somebody. Happily they walked to the nearest sand dune and sat there, grubby and sandy, licking their ices.

During the rest of the afternoon the school children paddled or bathed; got together and played more games on the sands; did more shell collecting; then finally stopped, exhausted, for tea and cake. Then, all too soon, came the time to pack up and make a weary journey back towards the railway station, the biggest of the boys carrying the now empty hampers.

Tommy Palmer had once again latched onto Nancy. She didn't mind. It was a bit like having a younger brother following you around. She did notice that by the time they reached the station Tommy had gone very pale. Perhaps he was tired – weren't they all? Nancy felt that her head was beginning to ache and she felt a bit sick as the train moved off. Now Tommy had gone from pale to being flushed, and he too was complaining of feeling sick. The little pair sat together, holding hot sweaty hands, wondering what on earth was the matter with them. And too shy to tell a teacher. They made it home.

When the train pulled up at the home platform, the farm wagons were again waiting to take them all down into the village. Tommy Palmer was clearly ill. As one of the teachers came to him he was sick and collapsed into her arms. Nancy too turned green and another teacher took charge of her, just in time, as she fainted, yet still hanging on to her sticks of rock and the rag doll she had bought at the seaside.

At first it was thought that Tommy and Nancy were ill due to the journey, or maybe too much sunshine and ice-cream. But Mr McBride, a more understanding teacher, viewed the little pair with rather more concern. They were feverish. Each arrived home in a teacher's arms; handed over to anxious mothers with the sound advice to call the doctor if they were no better by morning. In both homes the night was long with much delirium and sickness. As well as the headaches both Tommy and Nancy began to shiver and complain of sore throats. When Dr Grey visited both households he found children with 'white strawberry tongues', there was also high temperature and the early rash of scarlet fever. Was this the start of an epidemic?

Dr Grey telephoned the Matron of the local 'fever' hospital at Sutton-St.-Stephen. This only opened its forbidding doors for certain types of infectious cases which had to be nursed in a state of isolation. In turn Matron sent her maid off on a bicycle to find the ambulance driver, and within the hour an ancient ambulance growled over to collect Nancy and Tommy and transport them to the horror of isolation.

The accommodation at the hospital was stark and frightening. Sheets soaked in Lysol hung over the doors and there was lots of very intensive nursing. Worst of all for Nancy was the removal of her favourite night-dress and her new rag doll. The special sea-side rag doll. When she was told all would be burnt, her tears flowed, but Matron sternly ignored her pleadings to keep the doll. It was 'a dirty infectious thing' Nancy was told. She thought of Tommy, but could not see him. In fact he was not quite so ill, and was not at all bothered at having his old patched pyjamas replaced by a new pair. Tommy was, if anything, better off.

Dr Grey still had charge of his little patients. He came and sat with them asking all sorts of questions, noting everything with the skill of a good family doctor. He was collecting all the evidence to try and discover if this was the beginning of an epidemic in the village. He hoped Nancy and Tommy might be just two isolated cases – it was possible depending on the source of the infection. In the next four or five days if more cases appeared he would know what the community was in for. But by a stroke of luck no other children went down with the illness. Also, while there were no other children in Nancy's household, the Palmer family was vast, yet none of Tommy's brothers or sisters succumbed to the disease.

Within a week Tommy Palmer was well on the mend, apart from a residual cold. As he improved he was able to talk more easily about the trip. And one thing he did say was how he and Nancy Walton had had ice-creams. Nancy had bought him the last one in the 'man's box'. An idea formed in Dr Grey's mind. It was just possible to pick up scarlet fever from ice-cream contaminated with the germ streptococci, other than by the usual airborne way of transmission. A rarity, but perfectly possible based on the history of the two cases. Indeed Nancy confirmed that there were no other children buying ice-cream from this particular vendor. Thankfully Nancy, who was still very poorly, did not understand what her act of kindness had led to.

Unfortunately when Mrs Palmer heard that the ice-cream was the likely cause of her boy's illness she was straight round to Mrs Walton and gave her a verbal lashing. Nancy had no right to buy the boy 'mucky' ice-cream. And what did she think they were – charity cases? Tommy could have died. In truth he was very much better than Nancy, who did not seem to be improving.

Mrs Walton was very hurt by all the accusations. As she understood it Nancy had spent her last penny on Tommy. A kindness. Sadly the outcome for both little children had been dreadful. Even so Mrs Palmer made sure the whole village soon heard of Nancy Walton's irresponsibility.

In time Tommy was discharged home from the fever hospital. A week after this Nancy appeared to be on the mend and she too was allowed home from that frightening place. She was still very weak so Dr Grey kept the child confined to her bed. He visited her at least twice a day, for Nancy had become very breathless. She felt as if her heart was bumping in a funny kind of way. Lying propped up in bed she drifted in and out of sleep. It was an uneasy sleep, yet she had some lovely dreams of the seaside.

Dr Grey took Mrs Walton on one side and explained to her that Nancy had developed that most feared complication of scarlet fever – pericarditis. An infection of the heart. It would be a very long time before she could be considered 'better'.

The doctor tried all the medicines at his disposal. On one occasion even strychnine combined with digitalis. Later Nancy developed distressing sickness so the digitalis had to be discontinued. Dr Grey felt she would be best back in hospital, but Mrs Walton was frightened this might prove too much for the child. She would nurse her daughter at home for however long it took. It was agreed and that kindly doctor, always thoughtful of his patients, especially so those less well off, even provided a little bottle of brandy and – luxury of luxuries – one of champagne, which he thought would help.

Mother and daughter had much time to talk when Nancy was not too tired and gasping. And that talk was often of the trip to the seaside. Nancy's greatest sadness was that her rag doll, so eagerly bought with those bright pennies, had been destroyed during her infection. She also told Dr Grey about this and he was quietly moved by a distress that might have appeared unimportant to the grown-ups. To Nancy it was the saddest of matters.

One evening Mrs Walton was reading Nancy a story when there came a tap on the door. When she opened this no-one was there, but propped up against the lintel was a brown paper parcel. The sound of running feet was heard in the lane. Mrs Walton just caught sight of the mysterious postman. She felt sure it was Tommy Palmer.

Back in Nancy's bedroom Mother placed the parcel on the bedspread. The excitement was tantamount to Christmas Day. Eagerly Nancy undid the wrapping. To her amazement the parcel contained a little rag doll. It looked a bit like the one she had lost. Was it a present from Tommy? Mother said nothing but thought this was a likely conclusion. But why? Especially when such unkind things had been said and accusations made. And where would Tommy have got the money for such a present?

Nancy cuddled the doll. It was, if anything, a more substantial doll than the one to which she had treated herself. Its dress smelled of lavender bags. Yet it looked to be new. Mrs Walton was sure that she had seen the doll before – but where? The lavender gave her a clue. In one corner of the village shop window there was an assortment of items. The doll – with some lavender bags – had been amongst these. She remembered too that very afternoon she had seen Tommy Palmer with his nose pressed up against the shop window. Standing next to him was old Dr Grey. Had perhaps that dear man helped Tommy to secretly make amends? Mrs Walton would not have been at all surprised. Not that little Tommy had ever done a thing wrong to Nancy. It was his mother who had so misinterpreted everything that had happened.

When the time came for Nancy to settle down for the night, Mother gave her some medicine and a little brandy, positioning the girl in bed as Dr Grey had instructed. Nancy was so very tired yet still cuddled and kept smiling at her new doll. Before she slipped into sleep she once more spoke of the seaside. She asked her mother if she could have one of the sea shells she had brought back with her. Nancy wanted to listen to the sea again.

Staring at the peeling ceiling of the cottage bedroom, now mostly in darkness except for parts of it lightened by the shaded oil-lamp and the glow from the dying fire, Nancy said she could hear the sea again and see the blue sky with all the scurrying, billowing white clouds. Through these the sun was shining and the sea gulls were screeching and swooping. She said she was warm and so happy. And there was a very happy look in her eyes, but a distant look too. Her mother suddenly became cold and frightened. She understood what was happening.

As she was trying to think how to get help – help came. A knock at the door, despite the lateness of the hour. Mrs Walton rushed to open it. Thank heavens there was Dr Grey on the step. He was passing, had seen the light still burning in the bedroom and called in case all was not well.

Sitting by Nancy's bed Dr Grey watched helplessly, with the dreadful feeling he knew only too well. As for little Nancy, now she was back on the beach with sand trickling between her toes and sunshine on her face. She had the energy to run down to the sea shore and the gentle lapping waves. It was all so glorious. And in her pocket were six bright pennies.

1925 – A New Family Doctors' First Christmas

Donald Craig turned the final screw to hold his new brass plate in position on the sturdy wooden base, from which his predecessor's had been removed with mixed relief and sadness. It was the late summer of 1925 and Donald had at last fulfilled his long held ambition to be a family doctor; this after serving in the horrors of the Great War and the extra cruelty of the Spanish influenza pandemic that had followed in 1918/19. Both ghastly events that had claimed the lives of millions worldwide.

Late summer sunshine now lit up the plate and brought joy.

"It looks wonderful my love" a voice from behind him exclaimed. It was Jeanie, his stoic, lovely wife. Donald could only smile. A lump in his throat held back words of joy he wanted to express.

The brass plate read; Dr. Donald Craig M.R.C.S. (Eng) L.R.C.P (Lond) Physician and Surgeon

Donald's late father had been a consultant surgeon in London and had left his only son comfortably off, with separate provision for his medical training and to set himself up in whatever practice he so wished. Thus he had chosen a proven general practice, plus the retiring doctor's house and what was called the 'goodwill' – the established patients, let alone those on the 'Lloyd George Insurance Act Panel of 1911'

* * * *

Donald thought he would be visited or called out that evening, but it seemed that he was probably still being 'considered' by the patients…that was until the night bell rang furiously just as he was thinking of following Jeanie upstairs to bed. It was half past eleven.

Rain had come bringing with it a 'raggedy' boy of around ten or eleven. Donald was pleasant through his weariness. The boy was named Billy Suggs and was there 'cause his father- said to be Albert Suggs was 'reet badly again.' Possibly from a very full description of his symptoms, in left heart failure. When Master Suggs added "I think it's called 'cardiac' something!" Donald pulled on a heavy coat; took his emergency bag from its newly designated place in the hall way; called up to Jeanie he was off out, and followed the boy into the wet, dark night.

Very fortunately the Suggs family lived just around the corner of the next road, and they both hurried down a narrow passage between back-to-back houses. A sallow looking woman of indeterminate years hurried Donald up a stair case with a thread bare carpet. The sight that confronted him was that of a night emergency 'par- excellence'. Mr Suggs was sitting propped up across his bed, gasping for breath with bloody froth pouring from his nose and mouth. Classically, he was greatly cyanosed – his face lips and ears a blue/grey hue. His heart was in 'left ventricular failure' and his lungs were filling with fluid like a drowning man. Donald opened his bag and filled a hypodermic syringe with a mixture of morphine and atropine which was adeptly injected intra-muscularly. Other drugs such as digitalis could be given when the first 'shot' had quickly started to work, for in cases such as these, speed was of the essence.

Donald Craig gave a sigh of relief when Mr Suggs began to breathe more easily. Donald ascertained that he had not received any digitalis for his heart problems in the last two weeks. Indeed Donald's predecessor had not prescribed it in Mrs Suggs' memory. He had once been 'bled' to good effect during a previous attack of his 'cardiac asthma' – effective indeed, but not one of Donald's favourite methods except when all else failed. So he gave a small dose of digitalis by intravenous injection, and then listened to his heart. All appeared considerably better. When he could speak more easily Mr Suggs, recently so close to death asked a pertinent question. "How much will you be charging us for all this Doctor?" Donald exhausted with his efforts merely told Mr Suggs not to worry about all that now, but to rest. Outside the bedroom door Mrs Suggs asked would it happen again. Donald Craig was truthful. "I will try and sort out his heart problems for a short time with medicine, and then perhaps send him to a heart specialist at the hospital out patients, but I cannot say when, rather that if he has another attack; I will always come, day or night." He hoped he had shown himself in a good light, yet thought to himself here was going to be 'one of his regulars!'

* * * *

With what seemed great speed summer all too soon turned to autumn and then busy winter was on the practice. Donald and Jeanie had settled in and had become welcome in the area. For the most part the patients who had come along on occasion for medical advice seemed a pretty reasonable lot; no grumble ever reached Donald and the work was sometimes busy, but no more than he had expected. The Lloyd George Panel increased, as did the "I'll pay you now doctor, and then it will be done!" people. Namely three shillings and sixpence for consultation and medicine on the day. Some people who were struggling financially came to their own arrangements with Donald, yet he felt that these financial constraints spoilt the doctor/patient relationship.

Donald Craig soon became known for another aspect of family practice. He was said to be rather good at bringing babies safely into the world. He had what some referred to as 'the knack', and local mothers 'to be' were never shy nor hesitant to consult him early on when they were pretty sure they were expecting a baby. This was also time when he put aside one afternoon a fortnight for a special ante-natal clinic conducted with the local midwife Miss Finch who, glad to have a doctor who enjoyed this aspect of his work and looked at it as a joy rather than a worry or an inconvenience. Miss finch kept a regular eye on her 'ladies in waiting', reporting anything that gave rise for worry or that might foretell obstetrical problems at the birth. Donald's heavy black 'midder' bag was always fully prepared and ready to hand. Miss Finch rode what was patented as a 'midwifery bicycle' with special fixtures – fore and aft - to accommodate all her equipment and sundries. When he first saw this Donald stifled a laugh, for it reminded him of the 'midder clerk's' bike used by students at his teaching hospital. A truly well worn machine held together with surgical strapping and thick string. It had conveyed men of varying weight and size to home confinements in the

Paddington district, in all weather, day and night. It was pretty well moribund; coming to the end of its working life and was certainly not for the faint hearted cyclist.

Domiciliary midwifery was an important part of a family doctor's life in those days, for he was called in when 'nurse' was attending someone else, or most certainly when she felt that 'forceps" would be called for or the baby was unexpectedly a 'difficult lie'. The midwife always had to call the doctor in if any fancy needlework was required after an episiotomy. While babies could arrive at the most inconvenient moments, one could know that a 2 or 3 guinea bill would have to be charged, even if payment was made in stages. There were certainly no difficult births due before Christmas.

While Donald Craig was musing over matters obstetrical, he did recall one of his more frightening moments in his time as a 'midder clerk', nor was it the mother that gave rise to it. In days long past, two of the earliest types of anesthesia were chloroform and ether. Either could be used in a painful labour. (When Queen Victoria agreed to 'trust' the 'chloroformist', this became the most fashionable!) Both being in liquid form either could be 'dripped' from a specially designed bottle onto thick layers of gauze within a metal face mask. (Such were also used in general surgical procedures.) Using ether or chloroform great care had to be taken for they were very volatile substances, easily prone to bursting into flames should excess heat or flame come near. A spark from a fire in a bedroom was known to be lethal. The fright of Donald's life had occurred when he was taking a bottle of ether from the midder bag just as Grandmother appeared in the bedroom with a shovel of flaming coals red hot from the kitchen range, to replenish the bedroom grate. Very luckily the stopper had not yet been taken out of the bottle for use. A disaster was averted, but it had been – back in those student days a good practical lesson, and one backed by his obstetric 'teachers.'

* * * *

Christmas 1925 was fast approaching. Although he had only been in general practice about five months, and patients seemed to be 'constant', the financial position could have been better. If only some of the larger accounts had been settled by now it would have been easier. For Heaven's sake one of his slowest payers was a bank manager with high blood pressure and a neurotic wife who demanded Donald's ministrations - with medicine – nearly every week! In truth Donald was always worrying when he had no need, particularly about money even though his banking business was sound. Unlike some men of his ilk, he had a good personal account; a 'practice account' which always covered the monthly bill from the drug suppliers and those firms he had accounts with for practice equipment. Lastly there were lodged at the bank – for safety, all the shares and other securities he had inherited from his father. Few doctors – so early on in their career and having bought a practice so recently were in such a sound position. Even so with his first quarter- day (actually Christmas Day itself), he knew he had to seek a 'kind' way of chasing up un-paid debts.

As Donald was still writing up some notes in the surgery on Christmas Eve afternoon, Jeanie brought him a couple of mince pies and a cup of tea. She also had the afternoon mail. It had been mostly cards and one or two invitations to 'drinks' with other local doctors. The Craig's knew they should mix socially with the local medical establishment, but at this juncture only knew of a couple, or three other doctors in family practice nearby. However another simple greetings card, to which was attached a business card caught his immediate attention. It read: 'J J SMITHERS (late of the local police) DEBT COLLECTOR AT YOUR SERVICE. REASONABLE RATES. PROFESSIONAL HANDLING OF ALL MATTERS.' A local telephone number followed. He had heard that general practitioners did use reputable debt collectors for the must stubborn of non-payers. And perhaps Mr Smithers had heard of the 'new doctor in the neighbourhood'. He was worth a phone call with the last quarter day for 1925 upon him.

* * * *

As the Craig's sat down to a lovely supper at about 8 o' clock the surgery bell rang out. While the evening surgery had brought a few patients, Donald wondered if their evening would remain the same, yet this caller looked a sorry sight. A very small girl stood on the door step still on tip toe with her hand tugging at the bell.

One glance at the child showed she was ill and must have been in great pain. Just why she had come alone to the doctor, Donald could not think. He literally carried her into the surgery and placed her on an old arm chair that was usually offered to relatives whom had come with children or nervous patients. The poor little mite had a huge swelling on the side of her head, behind her left ear. This was clearly a very inflamed 'mastoid'.

The child's name was Mary Major, one of seven children, fortunately who lived - like the Suggs family close by the surgery. She was very tiny for a 6 year old. Mary said quite proudly that her mother often let her go to places on her own, obviously even to see the doctor. She had an ear ache for days and so the infection must have burst through the ear-drum and into the air cells that are in the makeup of the bone known as the mastoid process below each ear. Why Donald thought, did the parents let the poor mite suffer for so long? And why did they not bring her to him. Now with the increase of the infection she would require an urgent operation on the mastoid. Mary had a raised temperature and fear of complications. He called for Jeanie who straight away ran down the road to find Mrs Major. She was at home but had clearly been celebrating early. As Mrs Major was in no state for a trip into town, the resourceful Jeanie got a scrawled note of consent to take her place in the trip to the Children's Ear, Nose and Throat emergency Department. Donald telephoned the E.N.T House Surgeon on duty and as the hospital made ready for the child, Donald and Jeanie got her into the car and made haste up to there. Poor little Mary Major was a very urgent case, thanks to her parents lack of interest!

* * * *

Mary Major did require urgent surgery on her badly infected mastoid if there was to be a happy outcome. Donald had seen too many children brought to him for treatment, with some parents leaving it until the child was literally banging their head on the nearest wall to try and take the pain away. Mastoid infections led to deafness or even death from blood poisoning if not caught in time.

They paused again en route for hospital, to impress upon the parents how serious the case was. All the feckless pair in their Christmas drunken stupor would do was mutter that they would go up to the hospital later; but YES the doctor could take their girl.

The drive home was muted. Donald prayed he had not lost a patient, but in truth had done all he could 'pro-tem'.

On their arrival home Donald and Jeanie found a few regulars clustered round their surgery entrance, despite the hour. Even these folk should have thought that on Christmas Eve their doctor would be hoping for a break. Jeanie observed that they did not look ill; in fact there was a festive air about them. Many with smiles bore parcels and packets. Then it dawned on 'the doctor', they had gifts for the man and wife they had come to trust. Donald and Jeanie got out of the car. "Well now" he said, "who is sick this Christmastide?" Laughing broke out and hands were shaken. "Come into the waiting room, "Donald said. "It's jolly cold outside 'the stable'!" then a sense of shyness was followed by a hurried exit after each gift was given. "A token of thanks and appreciation for your care" Came the usual utterance as the gift was pressed into the hands of the Doctor and his dear wife. Jeanie seemed to have enough 'soap and talcum powder' to see her through the coming year, Donald was given lots of cigarettes and pipe tobacco, yet did not like to tell the well-wishers that he rarely smoked. And there was much else in the way of sweets and even food stuffs. Soon these well-meaning patients went quickly on their way to the local public houses for a festive drink, or home to prepare for the next day.

Donald had just locked the surgery door, when the night bell rang out. The caller was young Master Suggs. His father was having another attack of 'cardiac asthma' and mother had said it was worse than ever. For the umpteenth time Donald took his bag, checked it and strode out into the night. This time even morphine and hyoscine did not seem to work, so Mrs Suggs largest bowl was used to receive a large quantity of venous blood through old fashioned venesection, still an effective treatment to relive the congested lungs and failing heart.

As Donald eventually thought it safe to leave his patient with advice and medication, he felt it wise to tell Mrs Suggs the out-look was not too good. Again he said he would always come when called. This was not making more work for himself. Comforting words did much to ease the illness no matter how dire the prognosis. 'To comfort always' was a piece of advice given to Donald by his father, for whom it had often been the bedrock of his skill. It was clear that Mr Suggs in his condition could not live much longer, but he deserved hope at least. The left ventricle of his heart was clearly in a bad way, as were his so often soaking lungs.

When he got home there were no more calls for his help and to his shock Donald saw it was nearly midnight. He gratefully drank the tea Jeanie poured, and only noticed all her hard work with the Christmas decorations. The parlour looked very festive. As the mantle clock chimed twelve, the night bell joined in! On the door step stood Mrs Suggs. Donald's mood sank, but Mrs Suggs had a worn smile upon her face.

"I am sorry, "she said. "In all the business with 'Suggs' I forgot to give you the little gift he had for you." She handed over a huge turkey. "Suggs got it fresh from the market today, with our best wishes."

With this she turned to hasten home. Jeanie said "I think we are accepted dearest."

Donald held her tight. "It is a right fine feeling."

They made for the parlour again. And the telephone rang. It was his regular patient the Bank Manager's wife. She had chest pain. Jeanie giggled!

1936 – Here is a Wireless S.O.S. For Mr George Muir

Sir John Owen, Professor of Paediatric Surgery at St. Martha's Hospital, listened to the heavy down-pour of rain against the window, as he prepared for bed. It had been a long day, yet he was still Consultant Paediatric Surgeon on call, and inevitably the bedside telephone 'shrilled out'.

Sir John knew well that his Surgical Registrar, Mr Henry Morrison, would not call him except for the most serious of cases that either perplexed him or needed special expertise. Morrison was good – ready to sit his Mastership in Surgery. The telephone call was from this young man and concerned a two year old boy who had arrived in Casualty with clearly a serious 'acute abdominal' condition that most probably required immediate surgery. However there were a variety of additional problems that merited the attendance of a Paediatric Specialist.

Sir John's drive from St. John's Wood to the hospital was swift despite the weather. Casualty was quiet in the Children's area where he was met by Sister with a worried look.

"My goodness Sir John" she said, "This is most certainly the oddest thing, or should I say set of circumstances I have come across in a long time. Mr Morrison is carefully going over the poor little chap yet again to be sure of his diagnosis." She led the Consultant to one of the receiving rooms at the end of the Department.

Henry Morrison was clearly ideally suited to surgery both general and paediatric in particular. He was a tall young man with floppy hair and an easy smile that put patients at their ease, yet he clearly knew just what he was doing during his examination of a patient regardless of their age. As his Chief and Sister came into the room he politely greeted Sir John and thanked him for coming out at such a late hour.

"What do you think of our little chap then?"

"Well Sir" started Mr Morrison, "were I a betting man, which I am not, I would back intussusception".

Sir John stroked his beard, then spent a few minutes just watching the child's abdominal movement. "As the little fellow has got to know you, would you be kind enough to once again palpate so I can observe what immediately happens." Morrison gently did as he was asked, speaking kindly, reassuring the child all the time. There was one serious problem which made things very difficult, and which young Mr Morrison quickly turned and told Sir John just before laying his hands on the small abdomen. "I should say Sir that we know next to nothing with regard to any sequence of symptoms. The boy was merely handed over to Sister by a disinterested woman who made haste to leave. She had given his name as Alex Muir, aged two."

Sister Casualty politely broke in to say one of her Staff Nurses had in fact way-laid the woman, and with difficulty got a bit more information out of her. Sister had written this up on the Case Card.

As Henry Morrison was about to lay his hand gently on the little boy's abdomen the patient suddenly gave a scream and drew up his legs. A spasm had seized him; a contraction from right to left of the abdomen. His face was very pale. Very quickly Sir John Owen put his right hand on the abdomen. He could feel a small lump. Then the area hardened again and nothing was immediately palpable. He turned to his Registrar.

"I tend to agree with you old chap. Anything obvious when going along the line of the colon?"

"Yes indeed. As the spasm faded away I could certainly palpate an oblong mass. It was in the region of the hepatic flexure of the transverse colon. I thought it might be a very pronounced feature of intussusception." Both Consultant and Registrar knew this was now a serious surgical emergency and for a happy outcome an urgent operation was needed.

For a few minutes longer the two watched the child most attentively. Casualty Sister who had stayed quietly to one side now spoke up. "Should I alert Theatre Sister?"

"Yes please Sister, and get the rest of the duty team on standby. I think Dr Munro would be the best anaesthetist if he is on duty. He is superb with youngsters." Within a few minutes it was all 'go' and young Alex Muir was given a pre-med injection, and on his way to theatre.

Sir John, Henry Morrison and Sister went into the latter's little sitting room to assess what should be done administratively. Casualty Sister handed Sir John the Casualty Card with all details available and Henry Morrison's careful notes thereon. It would seem that what one of the other nurses had managed to glean from the presumed 'aunt' who rushed the child in but who had not bothered to wait, nor had given an address. She had said Alex Muir was merely a casual visitor when his father had to go away. There was no mother available. The only other clues were that Mr Muir was a stonemason by trade and had gone down to Cornwall to look at a job. The impatient aunt had murmured something about Penzance, and rushed from the department.

Sir John was, in these circumstances, happy to proceed with surgery, but would have to disturb the 'repose' of Mr Marsden the Hospital Secretary. This worthy gentleman would know how to get a wireless S.O.S. message out for Mr Muir, in time to be broadcast prior to the first news bulletin of that morning. Despite the early hour Mr Marsden took all note of Sir John's call and contacted the broadcasting people, who were pleased to help. The Hospital and surgeons were at least covered.

After a quick cup of Casualty Sister's excellent coffee the two surgeons headed for the Paediatric Theatre and the waiting abdomen of Alex Muir. Dr Munro had at Sir John's request used the lightest of anaesthesia for the job.

As they scrubbed up and Theatre Sister instructed a pretty little nurse (what they could see of her in her cap, mask and gown!) to 'dress the surgeons in their sterile attire', Sir John asked Henry

Morrison if he would begin the operation and seek inside for the source of the 'intussusception'. Morrison could hardly decline!

The operating theatre was its usual hub of orderly activity as the two surgeons silently came in. Morrison's heart was racing and his mouth dry as he stood before the small area of abdomen, draped in sterile towels. With a quick glance to Sir John he ventured "I think as it is ileocaecal I will open up with a paramedian incision?" Henry did not mention that he had already checked with Sir Zachary Cope's excellent textbook on the 'Acute Abdomen'. The consultant nodded in assent and the operation was in motion. The peritoneum was opened and the small mass of coiled gut located.

"Good man" said Sir John. "Now enlarge the incision a bit, then begin to try and uncoil the invaginated ileum that has crept up into the lax bit of caecum above it." Gradually it uncoiled, bit by bit. Sir John then said "You have done a grand job there Morrison. The final stage could be 'hit or miss' so don't be offended if I step in and finish the plumbing! It's a blighter to get back at the first go."

He did of course skilfully tuck everything back in the right order so young master Muir would be more comfortable and on the road to recovery, especially so if his father were located by the wireless S.O.S. message arranged to be transmitted after the first introductions to the day's programmes. It was carefully placed between the weather forecast for the day and the eight o'clock news. Sir John and Mr Morrison went to listen to the wireless set in the Ward Sister's sitting room, while she prepared them both poached eggs on toast.

Sister's wireless set was a splendid model in a walnut case with an illuminated dial. It soon 'warmed up' and was tuned in to the 'Home Service'. Then the clipped speech of the announcer was heard. "Here is an urgent wireless S.O.S. for a Mr George Muir from London, currently believed to be in the Penzance area of Cornwall. Can he please telephone St. Martha's hospital in Paddington, where his two year old son Alex Muir is seriously ill. Now here is the early news….."

Sir John smiled at Sister and his Registrar. "Good. That is that. I just hope to goodness he hears it. Or that someone who knows him or who, say, is discussing work with him, will pass the word on." Henry Morrison looked a bit glum. "What's up old chap?" the Chief asked.

"Well sir, while all went to plan surgically, since we left theatre I have a niggling feeling the little fellow might be sickening with a respiratory bug. Munro, when he was clearing up, remarked the throat was looking a bit sore, and he could hear at the end some chest 'creps'"

Sir John, as he was won't to do when debating a clinical observation, stroked his beard. "You went over his chest yourself in the initial examination?" he murmured to Henry.

"Of course sir…ears, nose, throat, chest. There was nothing to see – or rather hear – then."

Sir John made noises of reassurance. "Henry my boy, if you had not been such a good diagnostician and spotted the signs coming from the acute abdomen, by now we would be looking at a far more serious problem. Will you now go with the child from Recovery to the Paediatric Surgical Ward, and if all seems okay double check him and hand him over to Ward Sister."

When all this was done he thought he would go and get a proper breakfast, but leaving the ward he was waylaid by a Porter from the Lodge bringing him a telephone message. Mr George Muir had heard the wireless S.O.S. and would be on the next train to town.

* * * *

It would take Mr Muir perhaps six to eight hours to get up to London, even by express train. Henry was due to go off duty at lunch time, but he wanted to see the little boy's father and give him a good prognosis on Alex. He also had other youngsters to see and check over, but fortunately there were no more serious problems on the ward, although anything could happen.

When Alex Muir was truly awake Henry once again examined him bearing in mind what Dr Munro the anaesthetist had said. The chest was now certainly clear. His throat however appeared to be very red and raw. His tonsils were swollen and didn't look good. What Henry really wanted to know was if the child had any history of sore throats. This was something for a parent or relative to confirm.

For a good ten minutes Henry just stood by the cot and carefully watched Alex Muir. He laid a gentle hand on the little forehead, which seemed less feverish now. The child appeared as comfortable as possible. Henry turned on his heel, to find a young nurse quietly and neatly awaiting 'doctor's orders'. Sister had asked her to 'special' the child until he was fully conscious.

Henry was glad of Sister's actions, which were indeed the usual practice in such a case. He reflected a moment on the excellence of medical and nursing care expected and given to each patient. He then went over to Sister's desk, and finding Alex Muir's notes waiting for him, took them to 'Doctor's desk' in a quiet alcove at the end of the ward, from where he could glance up and look down at every bed or cot. Here, order was everything.

* * * *

When Henry had completed writing up the case history as it stood so far, he managed to go round and check Sir John Owen's other cases before the Consultant got back to the Hospital. Night Sister had by now gone off duty and was replaced by her day colleague. As all was quiet and well, Henry took a break to go and shave and bath; dress and grab a bite of breakfast in the Residents quarters. Should he be needed, a Porter would come and find him. Sir John Owen was preparing for his day in much the same manner. Yet as with doctors all over the land, no-one could truly foresee the day ahead, merely be ready for whatever came your way.

Henry Morrison, much refreshed, strode back up to the paediatric Surgical Ward at nine thirty am. Sir John Owen would doubtless appear, as immaculate as ever, on the dot of ten. When the Chief did arrive he looked, as always, the consummate Consultant. Dressed in black jacket, striped trousers and a pristine starched white shirt with a wing collar and conservative blue bow tie with white spots, his ensemble was completed by a gardenia in his button hole. Only when required would he put on a white coat. Henry too was neatly attired under his white coat, its pockets as usual containing all in the way of diagnostic instruments, note-books and two fountain pens, one containing black ink, the other red – for making diagrams in patients' notes. He also wore a bow tie. A wise move when doing both paediatrics with its vomiting babies and youngsters – and similarly if one was a Casualty Officer, when many a good hospital or university tie could be easily ruined!

When the ward doors did fly open and Sir John swept in, he had with him an equally distinguished consultant colleague, the great Mr Gilroy Innes, a tall white haired man with a military bearing and neat moustache. Sister almost curtsied before him! While Henry knew of this fine E.N.T. surgeon, he had never actually met him. He realised that Sir John had taken his worry about the bad throat of Alex Muir seriously. It was a good move.

On their way up to the ward, Sir John Owen had already told Gilroy Innes of Morrison's observational, diagnostic and surgical skills. How he had carefully assessed everything, hence the finding of a possible 'strep' throat, also remarked upon by the anaesthetist Dr Munro. Sir John, being Sir John, however emphasised the urgency of the acute abdomen, indeed their luck at so quickly finding the 'churned-up gut' and its successful unravelling and restoration in the correct manner.

Fortunately Henry Morrison knew nothing of Sir John's praise of him to Gilroy Innes. Henry did not rest easily with such verbal 'garlands'. He had won several prizes during his medical training, but not once referred to them. For a young and clearly 'up and coming' man he was modest at all times, so did just as he was bid and got on with the job. He was studying for his 'masters' in surgery and a Fellowship of the Royal College of Surgeons at the same time.

The three surgeons gathered round Alex Muir's cot. All spoke kindly and softly to him, with a nurse holding his little hand to reassure him. Certainly the 'intussusception' had gone the right way and all was in place with a neat and infection free surgical wound. Henry Morrison gave a quiet noise of satisfaction as the dressing came off. There was nothing in the way of pus thank God! Sir John smiled at him.

"Most gratifying gentlemen." He turned again to Henry.

"Now old chap, give Mr Innes the details of the throat situation. I see Sister has arrived with the appropriate trays."

The ward Ear, Nose and Throat tray of diagnostic instruments were sterile and ready on a small covered trolley. As usual, all was immaculate and to hand.

For all his military bearing and perhaps rather frightening persona, to the child, Gilroy Innes spoke like a doting grandfather. Without a murmur – which was rare – Alex Muir opened his mouth and let the Surgeon slip in the tongue depressor of the throat light. So adept was Mr Innes that the child did not even 'gag'. Only after examining the little nose, the ears, and also gently feeling the glands in the neck at the angle of the child's jaw did he pass comment.

"Well gentlemen, I have read Mr Morrison's pre-operative notes, and he gave full mention of the beginnings of a tonsilar problem brewing. Of course Dr Munro also passed comment on this at the end of surgery. However, the child's temperature has subsided. I feel it should be reviewed at the time of his discharge. If it has flared up again I will gladly have him up on my paediatric E.N.T. Ward and give him a good check-up – maybe a tonsillectomy if it is indicated. It would save getting him back later."

All three men were in agreement with regard to young master Muir, but there was still the matter of Mr George Muir's views when he arrived back in Paddington from Penzance thanks to the successful S.O.S. through the wireless.

Sir John Owen was a man of impulse, surprising as it would seem. After Gilroy Innes had left them, Sir John suggested that they do a ward round, re-arrange their day – God help dear Sister! And all so Sir John and Mr Morrison could take time to walk across the road to Paddington Station to meet the afternoon Cornish Riviera Express, and look for a worried man!

* * * *

At the station Sir John went to the Head Porter's office and asked if one of his chaps could stand on the platform with some kind of a board bearing the name of Mr Muir. This presented no problem. They had to hand a small blackboard and chalk for the very purpose; apparently quite a frequent request to attract incoming passengers.

The Riviera Express which had departed Penzance shortly after 8.0am came alongside the platform at Paddington at four fifteen in the afternoon. A tall porter came forward holding aloft his blackboard. As doors swung open and passengers greeted friends and relations, a thickset, ruddy faced man got out of a 3rd class carriage. He had but one battered suitcase and a workman's tool-bag. He saw the blackboard, and headed smartly for the porter. Sir John turned to Henry, smiled and said "Mr Muir I presume." He then strode over and introduced himself (leaving his Registrar to tip the porter!)

George Muir was a man with a quiet voice and very good manners. Sir John had been quick to introduce himself and reassure the man that his son was well on the mend. He did make a point of telling the little patient's father that it was Henry Morrison who had initially received his son and through excellent diagnostic skill had diagnosed a tricky abdominal problem needing immediate surgery for a happy outcome. Also that in such cases speed was of the essence. So it was that the three men entered the hospital and made their way to Mr Marsden's office where he could explain the rules regarding operating when there was no parental agreement.

They found the Hospital Secretary awaiting them and a welcome cup of tea being prepared, then they all sat down in an ante-room. And the story – the sequence of events – was explained to Mr Muir.

Sir John told how Mr Morrison, in charge of his admissions the previous night had been called down to Casualty to see Alex Muir. He had been brought there by a lady who was, it seemed, in a great hurry to go somewhere. At this time George Muir explained how Alex had been left with his spinster sister. He continued, "It was not an ideal situation gentlemen, yet sadly we lost the boy's mother eighteen months ago when Alex was a babe. At first my sister-in-law came down from Aberdeen to look after him, but she is a teacher and the school needed her back a month ago." As George Muir drew breath and sipped his tea, Henry quietly remarked "How very troubling for you Mr Muir."

Sir John then skilfully yet gently pushed the story forward. "I take it then that a job much suited to you came up in Cornwall?"

"Indeed it did" Mr Muir replied. "A fine stone-mason's business in Penzance, and with accommodation as a part of the contract, plus very good money for a skilled man. I was not too sure about taking a babe with me, but when I explained to the owner he said 'not to fret on it' for he had three capable daughters who would gladly work something out for us."

"How absolutely splendid" smiled Sir John. Then he asked "Incidentally, how did you hear our wireless S.O.S? It really was an inspired move by our friend Mr Morrison here." To which that kindly modest gentleman grinned with embarrassment!

George Muir explained "We were at the breakfast table and also listening in for the weather and the early news. Then to hear my name! Well, fortunately there was a telephone in the house which my new boss – I had got the job there sure enough – said I should use, to get on to St. Martha's Hospital straight away. Then I managed to catch the Express to London. The boss even rushed me to Penzance station in his van. Right good folk they are. And the job is safe too." He smiled, then asked "Was the poor little chap's operation really serious?"

"Indeed it was" stressed Sir John. "You see, if a youngster is admitted without a responsible relative in attendance, first we are obliged to try and trace one, or get legal authority to go ahead with whatever treatment is called for; in Alex's case operative surgery." He turned to Henry. "Mr Morrison, would you be good enough to frankly explain to Mr Muir the state of affairs when his son was brought into Paediatric Casualty very late last night, before you called me in that is." Henry nodded.

"I happened to arrive in the Department and saw little Alex on a trolley – a Porter had lain him there on Sister's orders. He was clearly very ill. I am sorry to say there was some, should one say, 'friction' with a lady, who seemed in a rush to get away. "I cannot be doing with him" she said. Fortunately Sister did get a name and address from her, and the child's age. She then rushed out into the night.

George Muir sighed and looked embarrassed. "That must have been my cousin Agnes. A strange, impatient soul I fear."

"Well now" said Sir John, "I think it is time for us to go up to the ward and see your son Mr Muir."

* * * *

Sir John made a quick call to the Ward Sister to make sure all was well, and young Alex Muir could have a visitor (it was said that Sir John Owen was the most courteous Consultant in the Hospital despite his elevated status). And so the three men made their way up to the Paediatric ward without due ceremony.

Alex Muir was lying propped up in his cot looking at an elementary picture book given to him by Ward Sister, from a supply she had in her room. So engrossed was the little chap with the big bright pictures that he did not see his Daddy.

"May I go to him?" Muir asked Sir John.

"Of course" came the glad reply. And though very young, the little boy held out his arms to the familiar man he knew as 'daddy'. Sister drew the nearest screens round the bed, and with a broad yet tearful smile 'shooed' both Consultant and Registrar away.

Sir John placed a hand on Henry Morrison's broad back. "I don't think we need worry much about that throat infection 'pro tem', do you old chap?"

"Do you know, I have to admit it had slipped my mind since Mr Gilroy Innes reassured us" he replied.

Companionably they strolled down the ward on the lookout for new faces.

1941 – To Edith and Dick... A Son

Thursday June the 19th 1941 was uncomfortably hot; Edith Johnson noted this in her little brown diary from Timothy White & Taylors. She scribbled this snippet of weather information as she sat under a large chestnut tree in the local park behind the library. Edith was waiting for her husband, Dick, who was due to arrive from his Army base near Newark for a long weekend leave prior to another local posting. And sure enough she saw his smart figure coming towards her, a 'swagger stick' under his arm. He had said on the telephone last evening that he had some good news for her. Indeed so, he had been promoted to a Captain in the Nott's and Derby Regiment (The Sherwood Foresters). Three 'pips' were gleaming on each shoulder, complementing the three medals below these epaulettes – medals from the Great War, and the trenches of Flanders fields.

Edith waved back, at the same moment feeling a strange little movement that was yet unexpected!

This was all a bit of a contrast to their first meeting. In 1918 Dick and his family lived on Musters Road near to the corner of North Road. One evening, Edith whose home was on North Road was hurrying along to a friend's house for supper. She saw striding along the eldest Johnson boy, Dick, wearing the smart uniform of a 2nd. Lieutenant in the 'Foresters'. One arm – the right- was in a sling, his hand heavily bandaged. Edith and Dick were only at the stage of a pretty smile from Edith and a cheeky grin from Dick that would be enhanced by his striking blue eyes. However something happened this evening that literally brought them rather more close! An elderly car coming down Musters Road and behind Dick suddenly back-fired- one hell of a bang- but Dick, from force of habit, threw himself flat! Edith's shoe caught in the heel of his boot, and found herself sprawled across him. They paused for a moment to catch their breath, and then Edith began to giggle. "You certainly know how to give a girl an exciting time Dick Johnson! You see I do know your name." Dick meanwhile was 'one-handed' helping Edith to her feet. He was pleased he had not automatically come out with an army type expletive! "I'm so sorry" he said "I am afraid hearing that explosion I automatically dived for cover." "And I followed suit!" Laughed Edith. And so with Dick's further apology together with a tender smile they went their separate ways. Even then Edith knew she had first spoken to the man that would come to mean so much to her and to whom some years later she would marry.

* * * *

After demobilization Dick Johnson, like various Uncles took up law, and became articled to a firm of solicitors in Derby. It should be explained the Johnson family all followed the learned professions – law, medicine or the church. Each morning Dick set out for Derby but in the evening hurried back to leafy Nottingham suburbia to see Edith. In April 1925 he was admitted as a solicitor. Strangely enough all three Johnson boys started in their professions: Dick a solicitor. Charles qualified in medicine and the middle son, Henry was in Cornwall, a Mining Engineer.

In the middle twenties twenty three year old Edith with her fashionable 'bob' style haircut was a regular visitor at the local tennis club with Dick, and when the weather was decent the young couple would take country walks to the pretty little village of Plumtree where the pub was simple but very pleasant. Dick would have beer in a pewter tankard and Edith a ginger - beer shandy. In truth one cannot say the 1920's were a halcyon era, but many believed that the end of the War and the back of the Spanish Flu – which fortunately neither Edith nor Dick caught, (Edith's uncle died of it in 1919). Their future seemed more 'rosey' as time passed, especially so after Dick had been 'admitted by the Law Society'.

Edith remained at home and helped her lone mother in every way she could. And both were happy to see Dick on evenings he was not tied up with work preparation. Edith Cooper and Dick Johnson were clearly deeply in love with each other and after Edith's 23rd birthday on the 6th of January 1929 – Dick used to call her his Epiphany girl – he asked her to consider matrimony in say two years, when he was firmly established in his chosen profession. His future mother-in-law was emotionally moved, for Edith was so dear to her as they did much together and she was entwined round her mother Bella's heart. Edith was the youngest daughter. Her older sister, by this time was a professional dispenser and bookkeeper for a Doctor in Great Yarmouth.

The family also included two boys. John was the second born child a couple of years older than Edith, with David the youngest and at this time still at school. The eldest Mary, although working away from home now, had- when the other children were so much younger, been a great help with them, particularly so with baby David. It worked out that Edith and John were close when growing up, while Mary and David, with the greatest age difference, were similarly close. All in all they were a happy family and not without their worries, but for all that balanced and utterly respectable. Now in 1928 Dick Johnson appeared likely to whisk away Mrs Cooper's closest girl. Dick asked Mrs Bella Cooper for Edith's hand and she agreed to the union taking place in three years. In 1931 when Edith would be 26. However an engagement could be announced in the local paper, when the ring was purchased.

In town the best place to have morning coffee or indeed afternoon tea was a splendid store named Griffin and Spalding which looked onto the Old Market Square. Market Street ran beside it and there were many old established shops and a popular 'picture house'. When they both had a day free, Dick suggested they should meet at 'Griff's corner' in the afternoon. Before Edith arrived in town Dick paid a visit to the palatial hall of Lloyds Bank and made a substantial withdrawal from his savings account. As he left the bank he could see the attractive, diminutive figure of 'his girl' patiently waiting at 'Griff's' corner' opposite the bank. She saw him and waved happily.

"Are you taking me somewhere special?" Edith laughed. "Of course. Come on." Dick smiled taking her by the hand. "We do have to cross Market Street first." He led her to the window of the tobacconists and paused pretending to be looking for his favourite brand of pipe tobacco. "No, there is nothing here I fancy. Anyway I have a full pouch of *'Three Nuns Empire'*." Edith squeezed his large hand. "Darling what are you up to? I can tell you are teasing me by the glint in your eyes. Come on you rotter, spill the beans!" He turned and whisked her into a very 'posh' branch of a London Jewellers two shops up. In a trice they were inside. Greeted by a very superior assistant, Dick asked if he could show the young lady a selection of engagement rings to her liking. Edith could hardly speak for joy.

Edith knew that this event was on the cards a week ago when Dick told her they could have an afternoon in town, but she thought it would only entail a bit of window shopping. Now her eyes were glistening with tears of happiness, and a choice that had only figured in her most wonderful dreams "Madam's fingers are very slender" the jeweller remarked. "I would think something delicate yet eye- catching. Is it to be diamonds? I think very much they would really suit madam." Madam liked the idea very much.

The first engagement ring Edith tried on was a beautiful solitaire ring, yet she could feel it was not quite right for her. Dick told her to take her time until the right ring was on that all important finger. Further up the display 'pad' there was a very pretty, yet modest diamond ring with three small but good looking stones in what was said to be a 'milgrain' setting. Edith tried it on and instantly knew it was just right. She turned and showed it to Dick. He smiled and asked "are you sure?" "Oh very sure" Edith replied. Dick was not an emotional man, yet a lump came to his throat at the look on her precious face.

With the ring in its little oval green leather box, Dick and Edith left the shop for the crisp winter sun-light. Edith was so very happy she wanted to dance and laugh, and told Dick so. "Well darling" He replied "we cannot go dancing at this time, but we can go up the street to the Picture House and see the new Disney Cartoon film they are showing there. I will hold your sticky little hand and you can laugh until you cry away that build-up of tears." And she did.

* * * *

After the pictures finished on this happy afternoon Edith and Dick walked back down through the Old Market Square and across to a favourite restaurant – 'Kings'- on the Poultry. The doors opened onto a lobby, at the end of which was a staircase down to the long dining room. They were greeted by the 'Maître-d, who took them to a discreet table. Two menus were ready for their choice of dinner, meanwhile two dry sherries were brought to them, pre-ordered by Dick.

"Darling, you are spoiling me so much today." Edith said. "Of course my dearest girl" Dick replied, then whispered "I do love you very much and have done for ten years, in fact since the day we collided at the corner of North Road and you fell on top of me!"

They carefully ordered their meal, and then merely held hands until a smoked salmon starter was placed before them.

* * * *

Edith was not a great partaker of alcohol, but had just one glass of a decent 'hoc' with her roast chicken, while Dick ate good mutton. Following their main course Dick asked Edith if she would like a dessert and she chose a Peach Melba. Dick opted for the excellent cheese board. To suitability conclude their celebratory dinner they had coffee and a fine French Brandy.

Feeling very happy they stepped out of the restaurant on to Beast Market Hill and walked towards a taxi rank

* * * *

In the three years that followed Edith and Dick bought a house in a quiet suburb north of the city and Dick joined a Nottingham firm of solicitors, with a partnership in view. Their wedding was set for the 1st September 1931, by which time Edith's mother had rented a very nice house on a side road that led off the boulevard that ran past a spacious 'green belt that was known as the 'Forest Recreation Ground'.

The 1st of September 1931 dawned fine for early autumn. The church was less than a mile away. Edith was given away by her eldest brother John. Dick's best man was his middle brother, Henry. Edith would be attended by her dear sister Mary. Both looked very lovely.

At eleven am the organ struck up. Escorted by two clergy men Edith, on John's arm with Mary behind, made their way down the aisle to where Dick and Henry waited. Of the clergy men, one was Dick's elderly uncle the reverend Tom Johnson who had a 'living' near Lincoln. He was going to perform the actual marriage, by kind suggestion of the Vicar of the Parish Church. Dick had already joked with Henry that he hoped the old boy would remember which service he was at! (There had recently been an unfortunate confusion at a funeral!)

The booming of the organ's introductory music brought Edith to Dick's side, and the wedding guests and a number of their wide circle of friends settled down to hear the local Vicar begin the service. John acknowledged the question "Who givest this woman to this man." And placed Edith's hand on Dick's. And so on to their first hymn in the 'Order of Service'.

A Lesson – based on the story of the 'marriage at Canaan' was read by Henry Johnson during which Dick stifled a snigger at a thought of how his brother would dearly like to turn water into wine! Then came the business of the marriage conducted by the lovable 'Uncle Tom'. He performed this with immense love. Dick was a favourite nephew, whom the old boy had prayed for daily while the lad was at the front in 1917. Now to see him happily married to such a lovely girl, brought tears to so many eyes.

The organist played the final hymn and the main participants went to the vestry to sign the register. Then it was down the isle to the joyous strains of the 'Wedding March' (composed by Felix Mendelssohn who died at an early age whilst dancing!)

Once beyond the church door many 'box brownies' clicked away and at last Edith and Dick were alone on their way to the modest reception at 'Pentillie' where a splendid spread awaited them and their guests. The centre piece was a cake baked and decorated by Edith herself. She was very good at cakes.

The whole day went smoothly and was truly happy; with weather to match. The memory would remain with them forever.

At the end of the afternoon a select group of relatives and guests went to the station to see the happy couple off on their Honeymoon. As Edith stepped into the London train she traditionally threw her bouquet to the group. It was dear Mary who caught it.

* * * *

Thursday June 19th 1941

During her wait for Dick in the local park that very hot June day Edith had slipped into a reverie, thinking on all that had happened in the first decade of her married life. There had been worries and sorrows but, despite the 'second' war things were now more promising.

The 1930's had- for everyone been difficult years and Edith and Dick had both had their fair share of hardships. In some respects the coming of the Second World War brought security for Dick. Being still in the Army reserve list and a 43 year old solicitor, he would at least be a staff officer, most likely to be posted to the Army legal branch. He joined Edith and after a brief chat during which Edith mentioned that the heat was 'getting to her', they decided to go back to their flat about half a mile away, where they could rest and cool off. As soon as they climbed the stairs and unlocked their door Edith went to the bathroom and was sick.

"Are you under the weather my love?" Dick asked. It was a loaded question. He felt he knew the answer. The last time he had leave was back in May when he rushed back following the night of the 8th and 9th – a night of heavy bombing. Edith had been at the flat when all the windows were blown in. in this corner of Midlands suburbia 47 locals had been injured and 43 killed with high explosive bombs. 34 houses had been hit. When Dick arrived in a staff car he was shocked, and discovered Edith had gone home to her mother's, the area fortunately missed by the air raid.

* * * *

"I had a surprise when I was up at Ma's." She smiled. Dick was thumbing through a pile of letters. "Oh good, that's nice." "Yes. I seem to be having afternoon sickness as well as in the morning. Most distressing." He took a moment to realise! "If you mean what we have been waiting for so long?"

"Of course I do you chump!"

"Medically confirmed, one assumes."

"Yes. Dr Dorothea Mann is caring for me. She has been my doctor for years. Getting a bit close to retirement, but none the worst for that."

"And when is he or she likely to put in an appearance?"

"Doctor thinks around the second week of October. So don't you dare get an overseas posting." Edith was serious. "I cannot see that at present, not at my age. If I go out of the Midlands I would be surprised. There are a lot of 'naughty soldiers' kicking their heels around for the moment. It is not like the last 'do', 'here is your rifle now you can bloody well point it straight' you are on the next train to Dover." Dick gave Edith one of his cheeky grins. It had yet to sink in.

* * * *

During July and the beginning of August Edith began to feel more 'drained and ill. Dr Mann was a regular visitor to the flat, coming down from town after morning surgery. Edith's blood pressure was far too high for comfort. She felt fed up with having to spend so much time in bed. Dick had been posted to a village not too far away, he could easily get to the flat and stay the night, cheering Edith up and sharing in the making of the plans. The baby certainly seemed active enough!

September 1st was Edith and Dick's tenth wedding anniversary, a very hot day but tinged with hints of autumn. Edith sat in the garden waiting for a promised visit from Dick. He too wanted to be with her. His staff job was dreadfully boring; the whole damned war was boring for that matter. At least his army pay was quite good, yet claiming anything extra to which he was entitled to was fraught with forms to fill in and then done up with red tape!

When he returned to his North Nottinghamshire base, Dick had decided that he should take some leave, for he had little on that required his urgent attention. His last day with Edith had seen a visit from Dr Mann who was equally worried about a constant 'high' in both systolic and diastolic blood pressure. This was not a good sign for either mother or baby.

Mrs Cooper had returned home to 'Pentillie' after a few days with her brother and sister in Bournemouth. She knew of course that Edith had not been feeling very well of late but the baby was not due for another six to eight weeks. However on the 8th September she came down to the flat and found her precious girl in such distress she smartly whisked her up to home and called Dr Mann.

Dorethea Man was a sound family doctor who feared any sign of an impending obstetric emergency. She promptly telephoned the best Consultant Obstetrician at the local women's hospital. This specialist was a Miss Margaret Glen-Bott. And so an urgent domiciliary visit was booked for first thing the following day. Meantime Edith rested and was pampered by her devoted mother.

Miss Glen-Bott was a kindly, but 'no nonsense sort of specialist. Medical ethics dictated that in a consultation at home the general practitioner enters the house first and introduces the specialist. First to the relatives and then to the patent. Of course prior to this, G.P and Specialist had met and discussed the case, then proceeded to 'Pentille' in Dr Mann's car.

On arrival at the house the doctors first met Mrs Cooper who took them into the drawing room where they found Captain Johnson who had just arrived to see his wife on a few days leave. Miss Glen- Bott thought what a quiet, polite man he was, and a true officer and a gentleman. So Dr Mann took her chosen specialist up to Edith's bedroom.

Edith had 'butterflies in her tummy' as she heard the professional tread coming down the landing. Natural fears of what to be done to either her or the baby caused another wave of nausea to sweep across her.

Edith received Dr Mann and Miss Glen- Bott with a smile. Dr Mann offered some calming words as she introduced the specialist, patted Edith's hand and went and sat down with her back to the window.

Miss Glen- Bott put on her rimless spectacles and smiled with genuine kindness. Edith relaxed. To Miss Glen-Bott she did not look a well lady. If only Dr Mann had called her in a bit earlier. And now there was only one thing to do. Even that was risky. Two patients to consider. Miss Glen- Bott began a skilful examination. This first thing she did was to look at Edith's left hand and her wedding finger with its ring. She could not rotate the ring on her finger. Observation of this told her a lot. It was clear that the finger had swollen. Oedema, a prime sign of toxemia of pregnancy. The blood pressure was 150/95. Not frighteningly high but clearly on the way up.

Miss Glen-Bott made a thorough examination of Edith, particularly noting the history of headaches, ringing in the ears and a certain amount of 'loin pain which made one consider early ill effects on the kidneys. Dr Mann had often checked for albuminuria in the urine samples Edith had given her. Hospital was most certainly the place for Edith. A telephone call was made to her Registrar by Miss Glen-Bott and a bed would be ready for Edith after lunch.

After giving words of comfort it was explained to Edith that bearing everything in mind it would be best to make some more tests in hospital then bring the birth on and make it as normal as possible. All would be explained to her mother and husband.

* * * *

Despite it being a short drive, Edith, Dick and Mrs Cooper took a taxi to the Women's hospital. Even with Dick holding Edith's hand in the back of the cab it was an uncomfortable ride, causing more nausea for Edith. All were glad when they reached the large glass doors on the Main Entrance.

Dick paid off the taxi driver who wished them well. Inside the doors a smart hospital porter who, as he was wearing a cap, saluted Dick who was still in uniform. Seeing the man's medal ribbons an equally smart salute was returned. Such courtesies were always important, providing caps were being worn!

Checking the admission ledger the porter found a note from a Dr Boyce to say as soon as Mrs Johnson arrived she, when contacted, would ask a nurse to come down and bring them all to the seats outside the Player Maternity Ward, where she would greet them as per Miss Glen-Bott's instructions. All seemed very well organized and running smoothly.

When shortly Miss Boyce appeared she had about her a great charm, yet gave the impression of a young doctor's 'growing authority'. There was no doubt this young woman was very bright and would go far, Dick thought to himself 'as long as she successfully and safely gets us through this fearful ordeal is what matters.'

A staff midwife then appeared and took Edith off to her bed. Mrs Cooper and her son in law sat in the hospital corridor both feeling anxious anticipation of things to come, meantime a set of green screens were wheeled round Edith's bed and she was helped to get undressed, placed in a gown and made comfortable ready for Miss Boyce's examination. Edith was allowed a short time with her mother and Dick, until the registrar returned to the ward. They were told that the Ward Sister would come and take them to her office for a chat; then they could say their goodbyes and return at evening visiting time, unless she rang them to advise otherwise in the event of the induction of 'Baby Johnson' having already begun. Such was the 'form'.

After Edith had been fondly kissed goodbye by Dick and her very anxious mother, doctors and midwives did not waste any time. First of all Miss Boyce came and took from her a very full history – both general and obstetric. A few simple investigations were requested. Blood was taken for a full picture. Her urine seemed of equal importance. And every organ seemed to be palpated and/or listened to. Her blood pressure was taken three times. Miss Boyce even examined her eyes. When she was finished the Doctor washed her hands for the umpteenth time. Smiling she told Edith her baby was well if a little 'small for dates'. Miss Glen- Bott arrived on the ward a bit later and quietly listened to her registrar's clinical history. She then felt the baby's position on which much depended.

Miss Glen- Bott listened carefully to 'Baby Johnsons' foetal heart with a polished wooden foetal stethoscope which was not so cold to the touch as the aluminium type on the 'diagnostic equipment' trolley.

Miss Glen-Bott and Miss Boyce seemed happier with Edith's state of health. It was then suggested Sister gave her a draught of the midwives favourite, a mixture of Chloral hydrate and Potassium Bromide. It tasted foul but ensured a good night's sleep.

* * * *

Saturday September 13th 1941

At 6.00am lights came on and the ward began to stir and burst into daily life. Day staff took over from the night staff that had made their report on each patient. Only one baby had arrived in the night and was doing very well. The new patient Mrs Johnson had enjoyed a good night, but it would seem her baby was rather active which came as a surprise. Miss Boyce had been notified.

On arrival at the bedside Miss Boyce asked that an early urine sample be provided for immediate testing; that the results of the blood film done the previous afternoon would be to hand. She then had a few re-assuring words with Edith (but was not personally too happy about the fact that Edith's temperature and blood pressure were on the rise, nor that she had been sick in the night.) Miss Boyce asked for Miss Glen-Bott to be contacted and politely asked if she could come along, but the screens swung back and the shining morning face of this dedicated specialist appeared. She was also clutching the details of the 'bloods'. Smiling at Edith she began to feel the baby. It seemed there was some response to early contractions, and these were not the famed 'Braxton Hicks contractions' that made many a new mother believe labour has really started.

The maternity nurses were asked to give Edith a wash and bed bath prior to the doctors and midwives starting true labour. It seemed- thankfully that the baby was making its own way out, a rarity in itself, yet the presentation was right enough, yet it would be a fairly long and risky job, but born he or she must be. And the premature baby unit and team were ready for action.

Sister was asked to ring Captain Johnson and Edith's mother, just to keep them in the picture; however Miss Glen-Bott and her Registrar knew full-well they were far from being out of the obstetric woods.

While having a quick cup of coffee in the Doctor's room the two surgeons discussed the odds. "I rather fear renal problems are developing" Miss Boyce was frank with her senior colleague. "Yes we have to move fast." Came the reply.

At that moment Sister knocked on the door and came in. "Miss Glen-Bott; Miss Boyce, I have just taken another close look at Mrs Johnson. I really think the baby is stirring." "Has there been any adverse change in the presentation?" Miss Glen-Bott asked, still holding her coffee cup. "Baby still seems fine" replied Sister. "Certainly a prem, yet seems to be doing remarkably well. Mother I fear is another matter. Her temperature is still 101 degrees but the B/P is down a bit. And it is not the first one I have seen do this. "Miss Boyce and Miss Glen-Bott went back on to the ward. Edith Johnson was a bit agitated as to the baby's chances. She was swiftly re-assured, yet now was definitely time to move her to the labour suite.

A further examination of the baby was reassuring. Apart from this being premature it was behaving itself very well. All agreed that there was no need for the use of Oxytocin to speed it into the world. Edith really felt it was coming of its own accord, so it was agreed that a warm bath followed by the usual soft soap enema would suffice with regards to induction if such it could be called. The average length of time for a first baby to be born was said – as per the text books – seven to ten hours. As was usual in the second stage of labour the foetal heart rate tended to rise between pains. The position remained correct, then at last baby Johnson emerged, a tiny boy weighing 2 pounds and 8 ounces. The time was 8.30pm on the evening of the 13th September 1941. A very tired Edith wept with joy.

When the final stage of labour was over and all was well, Sister telephoned Captain Johnson and Mrs Cooper to give them the good news. And on Miss Glen-Bott's say so suggested that although it was past 9 o'clock they could gladly come over to see Edith and the baby. Sister in charge of the prem' baby unit said that her latest tiny charge was not on continuous oxygen – indeed he was a prime, if tiny 'yeller!' Edith could hold him for a brief time when the relatives arrived.

The touching scene that followed in due course brought a tear even to Miss Glen-Bott's eyes. Inwardly she still felt a measure of unease, asking Miss Boyce to keep a very close eye on things.

Edith looked blissful as she held the minute and newly named Adam Philip Johnson. Dick too fought back tears, and tried to mask this by filling his pipe but was told by Ward sister NOT to dare light it!

* * * *

After a more than generous amount of time for a prem baby, Edith and Dick were allowed to share holding their 'wee mite' who was taken- still creating a fuss- back across the ward and into the specialist accommodation where he would have to remain., in solitary state, and pampered by pretty midwives and maternity nurses. Meantime Edith had a nourishing drink and another check over by her splendid Specialist.

Sunday 14th September 1941

Edith awoke early on the day after Adam had been born and despite feeling rather tried and queasy, lay back and listened for cries from the prem unit – the one place allowed constant low lighting, with at this time of air raids good black out protection. Edith could hazily remember time during the night when a midwife gently checked her, or a maternity nurse silently took her blood pressure with a sphygmomanometer and stethoscope.

Edith's bed was one closest to Sister's desk on the long 'Nightingale style ward'. As there was always a midwife or Sister sitting there, or a doctor writing up notes, those beds on either side of this location were always reserved for the mothers - both ante and post-partum and who required special observation (N.B. this was the intensive care place in those days!) There was a telephone on sister's desk, which at night had its bell switched off, the ringing substituted by a minute but flashing red light, even so conversation was kept short and in hushed tones.

As the ward was beginning to stir and one lady was wheeled towards the labour suite by members of the newly appeared day staff, Edith began to feel very uncomfortable with a throbbing frontal headache. Then Miss Boyce loomed up by her side. She smiled, and then frowned. "I feel you are not too good today, of course you should be a happy soul". Edith said "I think I am going to be sick!" Swiftly a nurse appeared at her side holding a round stainless steel bowl with a handle on one side Edith promptly made use of it. Miss Boyce had the screen round the bed in a trice as 'Day Sister' came through.

After Edith's face had been washed and she was feeling more human, Miss Boyce asked a few pointed questions and examined her. Edith was frightened. Surely this could not be right? Sister tried to distract her, telling of how well baby Adam was doing, in fact he was being given his Sunday morning break-fast which he received with surprising gusto. Apparently all the staff of the unit were in love with him! In fact one sweet girl was going to knit him a tiny woolly hat for the little bald head.

As the kind Sister was giving such cheerful, good news of baby Adam's progress, Miss Boyce was silently thinking rather more sombre thoughts about Edith. Bringing the baby smartly into the world had undoubtedly been the best course of action yet the headaches, nausea and vomiting plus the continuous hypertension were signs of toxemia. The last urine test showed considerable amounts of albuminuria. The results of another blood test on a sample taken during the morning examination would give a more up-to-the moment picture. Poisons in the blood caused by waste products not being excreted normally pointed to ureamia.

A maternity nurse was asked to bring in Adam for a moment, if only to cheer Edith, during which time Miss Boyce had gone to the 'Surgeon's Room' to ring Miss Glenn-Bott and write up Edith's case notes. The buff folder was filling up. At the start there was joy. Now more ominous observations and comments were being added.

Miss Glenn-Bott was most concerned at Edith's condition. Thank God the baby had come safely into the world, and that his mother got to hold him beside her adoring husband. "I will take a look At Edith Johnson before I do my 10.30 round Ann. Anyone else none too good this morning?" Ann Boyce replied that all was well 'pro tem', then let Miss Glenn-Bott get back to her breakfast.

Sister suggested to Edith that it would be better to keep the screen partially round the bed for now, but she would have Edith in view from her desk while she wrote up the full night report. Edith remarked that she still felt sluggish and queasy but more than anything wanted to sleep. As Miss Boyce had returned to the ward sister asked if it would be a good idea to give 60 grains of Bicarbonate sodium every two hours, plus phenobarbitone ½ grain to relax her, the doctor agreed and wrote the prescription up on the drugs chart. Very soon Edith was sleeping like her own baby. Before she went off to sleep she remembered that Dick would be with her after lunch.

* * * *

Over lunch at 'Pentillie' Dick seemed rather quiet, yet he had never been a 'chatty' man, especially at the luncheon table. "Something niggling at you Dick? Grinned John, briefly at home from the cold Atlantic. Dick smiled. He had a lot of time for John, now a gunner on a corvette. He was glad to be home, not just to get away from the war, but to see Edith to whom he was much attached. He was going to see her and Adam at two, with Dick. Mrs Cooper was going in the evening.

Dick realized he had not answered John's enquiry. "Well, "he said, you know how difficult it is to buy toys these days!" "Indeed" John agreed. Dick continued! Well I am going to give him my 'Old Bill' doll; I can give it a good brush up." 'Old Bill' dolls were in many a Tommy's knapsack during the last war – Dick had kept his very safe. It was a commercial image of the famous Barnfather cartoon character of a grumpy old soldier. His catch phrase was "let's find a better 'ole" and usually uttered from a corner of 'no-man's land.' This was familiar to all troops at the front, with shells whistling over-head. Dick was pleased with his idea. Adam would not understand anything much now but it could hang on the end of his prem. cot. And the Sisters and Nurses would know who he was.

The silence was even more pronounced as Dick and John smoked their pipes while crossing the Forest Recreation Ground on the way to Peel Street. Sunday visitors took every seat in the corridor outside the maternity ward. Men were mostly in uniform, on leave; Dick remarked to John that thank God they had decided to come out what in all three services was known as 'mufty'. The trouble was Officers were continuously being saluted by eager young men of lower rank and whatever service, so neither man regretted his soft hat.

On the dot of 2.00pm the ward doors were flung open by sister who in a loud voice reminded everyone that only 'two visitors' at this time could see their relatives'. And NO CHILDREN under twelve could come in. Lastly there was to be NO SITTING ON THE BEDS!

As Dick and John approached, sister drew Dick to one side to say Edith was asleep and if he and the gentleman with him (whom Dick introduced as his brother in law) would care to come into the 'den' she would give them a progress report.

To begin with sister re-assured Dick (to her Captain Johnson) that baby Adam Johnson was thriving well, but he would have to stay in with them until he had reached 5lbs in weight. He was clearly getting stronger and had a loud pair of lungs. Apart from the prematurity he had no problems whatsoever. He had been examined by the visiting Consultant Paediatrician, who had said all his standard tests were completely normal. While this was very good news, Dick was anxious about Edith. He had naturally not expected to find her out of bed and with renewed energy. Sister however explained that that Miss Boyce had made a very thorough examination of her from both the post-partum aspect of things and the medical reasons for her early admission and bringing the birth on. Now it was thought that she was still toxic and her kidneys were not getting rid of impurities in her system as fast as they should. She mentioned the tests that had been sent off early that morning and the treatment that had already been started.

All this time John, who loved his sister dearly just held her hand. He even surreptitiously noted her pulse. To him it seemed strong. Edith stirred a little but showed no signs of waking up. Dick wondered what the hell they had given her. He wished his sister-in-law Mary would appear – she was due back sometime that afternoon. Being a 'highly qualified dispenser' she would be able to ask the right questions. Dick took his handkerchief out and gently wiped Edith's forehead. The skin was dry now was she a good colour. Dick and John kissed her, yet still she made no response. Just as Miss Boyce came on to the ward. She made straight-away for Edith's bed. With a singularly firm yet polite authority Dick asked the doctor directly just how things were. Miss Boyce explained matters along the same lines as did sister, but she knew here was an educated professional man; and an Army Officer into the bargain. He would certainly see through any mumbled medical waffle. "In truth Captain, both Miss Glen-Bott and I are pleased with the birth, but concerned otherwise. I will know better this evening when the results of the blood tests come through from the laboratory." "Thank you very much for you frankness Miss Boyce," Dick smiled "I appreciate all you have done for the 'little lad'. I know you will also do everything that is needed in my wife's case. I should tell you that my brother Charles Johnson is a rural G.P. as was my grandfather. His father in turn was a London Surgeon. If it had not been for the last war I would have possibly gone down the same path. It was a toss-up between medicine and law. I read law at Lincoln College, Oxford." He paused. "I'm sorry I must be boring you when you have other ladies to see. "Miss Boyce was not bored, she was fascinated. "I will be seeing Miss Glen-Bott and I know she will be seeing Mrs Johnson after visiting time. Are you coming for evening visiting, if so we can all talk about a prognosis?" Dick smiled again at the pretty doctor, as did John whom Dick hastened to introduce. "That would be a great help. Edith's sister is on her way up from Great Yarmouth where she is a dispenser-cum-bookkeeper for a G.P."

"Then I better make sure I know all that I have prescribed!" She laughed a pretty laugh and headed for her next cases.

Both Dick and John kissed Edith goodbye and made for the prem. Unit to see Adam, on strict instruction of sister.

* * * *

Once back home Dick's mother-in-law was anxious to hear the most recent bulletin on both Edith and 'the little one' Dick was truthful. Mrs Cooper took a deep breath. "Well at least Adam is very resilient bless him. But oh my darling Edith, oh dear me!"

She turned to John. "My dear I know you are so fond of her. You always have been since you were children." She then gave a gasp. "John I nearly forgot, an urgent PRIVATE telegram came for you while you and Dick were out. John took the buff envelope. "From the Admiralty. " Opening it he cursed, "Damn and blast it is a naval recall. I have to report back – should I say 'from whence I came by midnight. I have the train times. Ma be a dear make me a flask of tea, while I change and pack. He then paused for a thought then asked Dick, "do you think the hospital would let me see Edith if I charge back to say goodbye. Lord knows when I will get another leave. I can go to the station from the hospital?" Dick headed for the phone on the landing window sill to sweet talk sister or Staff nurse on duty.

Fortunately Sister had just returned to the ward following toasted crumpets and a jar of her country sister's home made blackberry jam, a little luxury she readily shared with her nursing and medical colleagues in times of hardship. She felt well with her small surge of blood sugar.

Taking the special call from Captain Johnson asking if Petty Officer John Cooper could rush back to see Edith because of his naval recall, sister readily agreed, telling him that Edith was awake, not that well but rested. To see her loved brother would do her good. Sister maternity was both sensitive and thoughtful.

John, despite his kit bag and small 'liberty leave' attaché-case with toilet and shaving items in it, made his way to the hospital at what Dick would have termed the 'double quick' The navy did not march at this speed. At the doors of the hospital he was met by a pre-student nurse who blushed, to speak to the handsome Petty Officer. She rushed him straight up to the ward where sister and Miss Glen-Bott stood waiting. John was duly made known to her. He explained that he only had about an hour before his train left the Victoria Station, but a short walk away. Sister said that Mrs Johnson had been moved to a private room just off the ward. Here also a nurse sat by her bed and gave her special attention. Edith was certainly awake but to John feared the look of her. She was very happy to see him, it being a nice surprise. "Have you seen our lovely boy John?" John said he had and he understood the little chap was doing well. He joked that Adam wasn't short of pretty girl friends. They laughed, this brother and sister who adored each other.

Sister came in and reminded Petty Officer Cooper that he had a train to catch! John bent and kissed Edith goodbye. Nothing was said about the next time they would see each other. It was considered bad luck in these times.

* * * *

On the station platform, for a while John sat on his kit bag then a bell rang indicating a train was approaching the opposite platform serving the up-line. It shed its passengers. Until the train opposite responded to the guard's flag and whistle John could not see many of the passengers who had alighted. Then to his joy he spotted a young lady he knew very well. It was Mary. She had arrived from Great Yarmouth. She had started to ascend the steps of the bridge across the lines, heading for the exit when she noticed a waving sailor that was her brother. It was a very pleasant surprise as she thought he was at sea. Coming down the opposite steps Mary waved an arm, the hand of which held a book. Mary was an avid reader of current fiction. She had been reading the latest 'Monica Dickens' during her journey. At last they were together. The conversation was brief for the bell announcing the approach of John's train. John said Edith was not too well but would be glad to see her big sister. As much as possible was said before they rushed their separate ways, and silently both wondered when they would see each other.

Mary took a Steamline Taxi from the station to 'Pentillie' and was greatly welcomed by her mother and Dick, who looked terribly anxious by the situation.

Ward Sister- always so caring and considerate had telephoned Mrs Cooper after John's visit to Edith and suggested that as Edith now had a room of her own next to the ward entrance, Captain Johnson and she could come whenever they wished, and yes of course Mary was welcome too. All this was said with absolute calmness so as not to give – at that time – any hint of things going wrong. Anyhow until Miss Glen-Bott had her late afternoon round at the end of visiting, there was nothing to be officially said.

Monday 15th and Tuesday 16th September 1941

When Dick, Mary and Mother had come to Edith's bedside on the Sunday evening as suggested by Sister they found Miss Glen-Bott and Dr Boyce going through the latest blood tests to come back from the laboratory. Edith was again in a deep uneasy sleep. Miss Boyce wrote a further blood pressure reading on the special chart. She knew in truth the lady was not responding to such treatment as was available.

* * * *

When on Monday Dick went to the side ward he found Edith slipping in and out of consciousness. She tried to say his name once or twice but he could not really be sure if she really recognized him, even though he was back in uniform. Sister could see his own quiet despair and told him to go and see baby Adam who was apparently having his feed with the usual gusto!

Each time Dick or Mary and her mother went to the ward, now virtually a second home to them, everything seemed to be in 'status quo'. On Tuesday evening sister took them all into her room and explained Edith Johnson was now not responding to treatment yet her heart and pulse were strong. Dr Boyce then came in to say her kidneys were failing and toxaemia had increased. She had developed uraemia and sadly there was no real hope.

From Tuesday until early on Thursday the 18th September Edith's coma deepened. Family members were given free rein to come to the side ward where Edith lay, as they wished. This applied particularly so to her husband. Sister grieved for him and the sweet little baby. He would, one day, in the future become a credit to his parents.

Mrs Cooper; her eldest daughter Mary and Captain Johnson stayed at the hospital until 2.00am on the Thursday, but at 6.30am Dick answered the telephone prior to any sleep. It was sister who had come on duty at 6. o'clock to take over from her night colleague, and looking at Edith Johnson saw she was 'Cheyne Stokes' breathing and the end was very near, so she had got Miss Boyce out of bed and had made the call to the Captain.

Dick Johnson reached the ward a few minutes after 6.45am. Edith had only just died. He took her hand and kissed it through silent tears.

* * * *

After the statutory cup of hot sweet tea with Sister, Dick went to be with his and Edith's son, sleeping peacefully after his feed and wearing a newly knitted tiny woollen hat. Nurse said with tears in her eyes, he could kiss the little chap.

* * * *

Edith's funeral took place only two days following her death yet all went smoothly and well. The mourners comprised only of those friends and relatives that could be notified and could travel in time. There were beautiful flowers in abundance.

Being a morning funeral, Mrs Cooper still managed a good buffet lunch, and Dick saw there was plenty of liquid refreshment, if only sherry sweet and medium dry.

After the mourners and finally departed with the usual final words of condolence, the immediate family spoke more openly about the sadness of it all and even how Mrs Cooper would manage when baby Adam would come home after he had reached the weight of 5 lbs, the usual criteria for hospital discharge. Dick was more than concerned as he knew he would soon have to return to duty as there was only so much compassionate leave given. Also there had been military 'mumblings' about him being posted abroad with the legal branch. Mary came to the rescue. She had arranged for another dispenser/book keeper to come in to the doctor's practice and do a long locum. So Mrs Cooper and Mary would take care of tiny Adam when discharged.

In the week following the funeral Dick felt he must go down to the suburban flat to check all was well with it. Turning the left hand corner by the Cricket Ground he could see the bay window of the first floor flat's front room. A shiver went down his spine and it hit him hard to know Edith would not be there to greet him. There would be no smile and wave for him. When he got to the front door porch his hand was unsteady as he struggled to get the key in the lock. The ground floor flat was vacant, ready for a new tenant. Dick climbed the stairs he knew so well and made his way along the landing, past the bedroom door to the empty front room. It was tidy as ever. A book rested on the arm of the chair, a book mark at the place Edith had got to. A book never to be finished. Then came a flash of something white protruding from behind a cushion. Dick bent and pulled it out. A ball of white soft wool, one knitting needle was safe in the ball of wool, while its partner bore the beginning of a bootee!

Dick sat in the chair in which the dearest girl in his life had last sat, had knitted and read and had, as he had been told, felt so ill she phoned her mother to come and fetch her. He had not been there. He felt empty, useless and so dreadfully sad. With his guard down, the stiff upper lip crumbled and momentarily the tears flowed. Then he yearned to be with his baby son, given to him by Edith. Dick composed himself by smoking his pipe. Then after a wash and brush up, he headed out into the September day – back into town and to the prem. Baby Unit at the Women's Hospital.

* * * *

POSTSCRIPT

This is a true story told for the first time. The medical aspect gives a real picture of obstetrics at the time, the emphasis being on toxaemia of pregnancy.

All the characters portrayed (except Edith) were very well known to me, and while all are now dead, I have still used their second Christian names for respectful anonymity. The surnames of the two families have also been carefully altered. This then is how their lives turned out.

Baby Adam thrived well much to the joy of not only the family, but the satisfaction of the Premature Baby Nurses. When he reached the weight of 5lbs he was allowed to go home to his doting aunt and grandmother. Mary made a great sacrifice and gave up her career to care for the baby. (This was not only the reason. Mrs Cooper had developed a malignancy, which Mary bravely coped with until her mother's death in 1946)

As he feared, Dick Johnson got posted to the Middle East in 1942, going to Palestine after months in Egypt, thence to Greece and finishing up in Italy, until his demobilization in late 1945. Back home Dick returned to civilian legal practice. He and Mary were married in September 1946. A second blow came when Mary died suddenly of a stroke in 1958 when Adam was sixteen. Dick became ill in 1962 dying in January 1964.

Of other family members mentioned, John survived the war after which he and his family went to Australia where he died in the 1970's.

The youngest brother, David, had during the war served with Fire Brigades in London, Coventry and Manchester, in some of the worst bombing seen in the war. In 1945 – after his marriage – he was posted to the Brighton area where he remained until his demob. David and his wife returned to Nottingham where the first of their two sons was born. David and his family remained in Nottingham. He died in 1991.

Adam was very close to his uncle who acted as his best man in September 1966 at a splendid Cornish wedding.

* * * *

MEDICAL FOOTNOTE

(i) I do feel that a special reference should be made with regard to the late Miss Margaret Glen-Bott who at the time of this true story was the leading Nottingham obstetrician and gynaecologist, whose skills were much in demand. (Hers is the only real name used by me in this story.)

A distinguished surgeon Miss Glen-Bott was the city's first female gynaecologist, actually coming to Nottingham from Bolton as a House Surgeon, in 1916, and remaining here until her retirement in 1968. She also played a great part in various aspects of public life from 1937. In 1956 she was elected an Alderman of the City. She remained a Consultant for 15 more years and spent time as Chairman of Nottingham No. 3 hospital Management Committee. She died in 1969.

(ii) I feel that here it would be useful to mention that after sepsis in various forms it was toxaemia that accounted for the next highest cause of maternal mortality.

The condition albuminuria is a prime warning sign and easily diagnosed in a routine urine test carried out in the G.P's surgery or Hospital clinic. Toxaemia may lead to pre-eclampsia – convulsions arising in pregnancy – or renal problems such as arising in this story. Regular urine tests and a careful watch kept on maternal blood pressure and for symptoms such as nausea and vomiting, headaches and fatigue are most important.

Source: Queen Charlotte's Textbook of Obstetrics' by Aleck Bourne FRCS, FRCOG. (Obstetric Surgeon to Out-patients, St. Mary's Hospital, Paddington)

* * * *

DEDICATION

This story is dedicated to the memory of my late parents and also my late step mother who gave up so much to love and care for me.

S.C.M 2013

Dick in 1917 prior to active service

Edith in the garden at North Road, West Bridgford, 1927

EDITH AND HER MOTHER'S HOME 'PENTILLE' ON FOXHALL ROAD NOTTINGHAM, SEPTEMBER 1931

JOHN ON HIS WAY TO 'GIVE EDITH AWAY', 1ST SEPTEMBER 1931

EDITH AND DICK IN THE GARDEN AT 'PENTILLE' AFTER THEIR WEDDING

MARY ADAM AND DICK, AT THE END OF THE WAR IN 1946

1948 – Dear Gerald

The young Doctor needed a change of scene. For two years he had been sitting on his behind as a medically qualified "rubber stamp" for what was then a County Health Authority; a job taken in the misguided belief that he would have more satisfaction serving the "community as a whole". This was not so. Life now consisted of mountains of official "bumph" and incomprehensible meetings. When not in a meeting he was composing long-winded memos which would be duly changed by half a dozen lay administrators to suit their purposes. The stuff he had supposedly written was then returned for signature prior to being discussed at further meetings and subsequently put on ice for an unspecified period. His stethoscope was gathering dust; he was bored stiff; developing a paunch; lived in fear of haemorrhoids and tended to fall asleep during the long dreary afternoons.

His cousin Tom rescued him from piles and cerebral atrophy. Tom was much younger and brighter than he and felt a kind of family affiliation in that he would always be on the lookout for suitable jobs for him. To date he had chosen at least three hospital posts for him, but this present work was of the Doctor's own choosing, hence its abysmal failure!

Apparently Tom had put his name forward as a possible long term locum for another GP friend, and he had been "taken up" so to speak. He didn't like to refuse, so off he went to the Lincolnshire countryside.

The job turned out to be a little gem. Four weeks in glorious August, caring for a small list in tranquil surroundings. Tom was a 'mate' indeed.

The Doctor's arrival at Netherwold was not as eventful as he expected in a sleepy country village and the few people seen about did not return the cheery smile from the car! They glared back at him, presuming he was just another sightseer come to disturb their rural calm.

The family doctor for whom he was standing in was a kindly, talkative man who told all that was expected of him at incredible speed. He then hurried him through from lounge to dining room for lunch before his departure on holiday. He was off as soon as we had finished the cheese, leaving him with vague instructions, an antiquated housekeeper and an emergency bag that contained a few instructions and emergency drugs which seemed to date back to the 1930s.

Contrary to first impressions it came as a shock to discover that the practice had in fact some ancillary help. This was in the form of Nurse Mabel Mort, late QAIMNS, the most dedicated of women. Yet there was a problem. Nurse had a surprising inability to communicate effectively on the telephone. Everything was said with clipped military abbreviation, at first very hard to understand. It was her habit to telephone the Doctor precisely at 0800 hours each morning with details of those cases she had already seen and which she felt he should be concerned with. Exactly how many patients were treated by Nurse and never got to the surgery one would never know, but there was no come-back and all seemed to work smoothly.

One morning, after the locum had been working steadily away for about a week, the telephone rang bang on eight o'clock. It would be the morning report! Nurse's strident tone rang out.

"Message from the Grange Doctor. Dear Gerald again. Had a turn at 0730. Won't come out of the greenhouse. Can't get through to him. Better come!" The telephone went dead.

Who on earth was "dear Gerald", and what sort of turn was he having? The Doctor decided to ask the house keeper who the folk at the Grange were, and it seemed they were named Haveringham-Sim. That was all one got out of her! The filing system in the surgery, for there were no computerised records in those days, shed little light on the family history. There was a G. Haveringham-Sim recorded. Aged 57. The card was blank. He must have been a very rare patient to the practice, and certainly there was no history of him having "turns". The Doctor asked where to find the Grange, and set off with a worried frown. What would one find?

In truth the Doctor was not very happy about what appeared to be a full blown GP psychiatric emergency. He frantically tried to recall long past lectures by learned professors. It was not a subject that had ever caused him any real fascination, so he had not paid as much attention as he should have done. There was something going through his mind relating to statements such as "be frank and honest at all times", and more ominous "make sure you have good means of escape"! Also "have adequate assistance at all times". It seemed that he was to be faced with an agitated middle aged man having paranoid delusions in the greenhouse. He did not like the thought of being surrounded by all that glass one little bit! But it was conjecture at this stage. Fortunately the old bag contained some big vials of chloropromazine which would knock the patient out if one could get close enough to jab the syringe needle into his backside. Then he could assess the situation and if necessary arrange admission to a psychiatric hospital under the relevant section of the Mental Health Act. He only hoped that Nurse Mort and any other people around would give 'adequate assistance'. Of course, the "turn" could be anything or nothing at all. He tried to kid himself as the car sped through the gates of the Grange.

The house was all the Doctor had expected. A Queen Anne Manor House in very lovely surroundings. The grounds were well cared for, but corners showed them to be beyond the capabilities of a middle aged couple with, he guessed, little in the way of domestic help.

With difficulty he found the front door bell and gave the brass knob a hefty tug. A bell jangled way down distant corridors. No one came, nor did they to a second and third time of ringing. Then it occurred to him that the household, with Nurse Mort, must be surrounding the greenhouse, keeping an eye on "dear Gerald" who was probably on his hands and knees amongst plant pots and fading blooms. Taking a firm grip of the medical bag he plodded round to what appeared to be a kitchen garden, and sure enough there was a greenhouse. The door was wide open and all was in chaos! Gerald must have charged out. For one ghastly moment he wondered if Nurse Mort and anyone else had been hurt. Perhaps Gerald, in demonic fashion was holding them somewhere. This looked very serious indeed. Perhaps he should go and call the police now, he thought. A voice called from some other part of the garden.

"Coo-eee Doctor. We are over here." Across the lawn he saw a white haired old lady of ample proportions. She was hailing him from the open French windows of what must have been the lounge. She waved again and came over like a dowager duchess in full sail.

"Nurse and Gerald are indoors now, Doctor. She has calmed him down a bit, but I am afraid he has got into the main bedroom and we think he is lying behind the door. Oh and he has taken his rag doll with him."

The Doctor's face must have shown stark terror at the situation. But Mrs Haveringham-Sim chatted merrily and seemed unperturbed.

"Of course, he's always doing this you know. Nurse can usually see him through it, but the old doctor and Gerald are such friends he will always come along when things get difficult. Just a few words from a pal seem to do the trick. We never have this trouble when George is at home."

"George?" he must have sounded completely gormless.

"Yes, George – my husband. He's in oil you know. Spends most of the year abroad."

If George was the G. Haveringham-Sim on file, who on earth was Gerald? A dotty brother perhaps?

They climbed a magnificent staircase. At the end of the first landing he could see the military behind of Nurse Mort who was bending down peering through a keyhole. Once beside her the Doctor said in hushed tones "So he has barricaded himself in there has he?"

"Yes. Damned fool. Needs a good dose of liquid paraffin. Keep him occupied and his mind off that stupid doll. Thinks he loves it."

He was rather surprised at Nurse's blasé view of such a serious situation.

"I think I had better get in and give him a sedative, but I will try talking to him first. It might work."

Nurse looked puzzled as he opened the bag and filled a large syringe ready for the time when he got through the door. Then he called out very firmly.

"Gerald, old chap, this is the doctor. Come on, open up the door and let's talk things through should we. Let me in Gerald."

"But he's up against the door Doctor." Mrs Haveringham-Sim was getting perplexed, and when he got down on his hands and knees she gasped in amazement. But the Doctor was listening, listening for any hint of distress. From behind the door he could hear nothing but snuffling and heavy breathing. Gerald sounded a bit chap. He tried talking again.

"I know I can help, Gerald. Just give me the chance. Come on, open the door." Again he listened intently. Gerald's breathing was strange. He hoped his burst of hyperactivity had not caused a stroke and this was Cheyne-Stokes breathing. It was all the more important to get through that door. What might greet him on the other side was something he would just have to risk. He turned to face Nurse Mort and Mrs Haveringham-Sim. They were a stony faced the pair of them. He sensed all was not well.

Had he made some dreadful professional gaffe? Still nothing was said.

"I will try not to damage your door" the Doctor said, "but I must get in immediately." The lady of the house looked even more horrified.

"If we can confront him face to face, then I think I might get him out of this situation relatively unscathed. I must, we all must, be firm. I'll get in and give him the drug. After that we will assess the situation."

Mrs Haveringham-Sim glared at Nurse, and Nurse assumed an expression of a Guide Leader having trouble with "Sky Lark Patrol", only Doctor sensed that he was that trouble!

"If we all push hard at the door Doctor, perhaps we can roll him over, make him move away, then you can bounce in and do what you think best." Mrs Haveringham-Sim suggested with a triumphant smile. He was a bit uneasy, but it might work, at least enough for him to get through the door.

Then Gerald started to cry! The Doctor called out again, urging him to be let him in, and he was so concerned he did not for an instant consider the nature of the crying. Nurse had her mouth open to tell him something, but he had lunged against the door, feeling it suddenly give on the other side as Gerald moved at the same time. The door swung wide and he fell into the room and found himself face down on the expensive Indian carpet. At the same moment there was a shattering of glass, and as he prised himself up he was horrified to see Gerald had flung himself through the window. It was frightful! Rushing over he peered down into the garden expecting to see a broken body below, while the two ladies breathed heavily down his neck. There was no sign of anyone, just a disturbed flower bed where he had landed and evidence that he had made a dash for the shrubbery.

Mrs Haveringham-Sim was the first to speak, and she was very cross. "Right, that's it! The silly fool can stew in his own juice for a while. He'll come back when he is good and ready. I suggest we all go down to the lounge for coffee." She promptly turned on her heel and led Nurse Mort and the Doctor back down the staircase.

Nobody spoke as they all sat and sipped coffee. Nurse kept giving Doctor looks as if to say "You've really mucked this one up", and our hostess seemed to have lost all interest in Gerald's "turn" and was earnestly discussing the forthcoming Parish Bazaar. It was a most uncomfortable time, yet for some reason he couldn't bring himself to start panicking about the patient's condition. At last he spoke up like a naughty schoolboy who has made a mistake, and he expected a good telling off from Nurse.

"Don't you think I had better go in search of Gerald? He might be hurt. Where do you think he could have gone to?"

"Oh he will be in one of his little haunts" Mrs Haveringham-Sim smiled. "Probably the old tack room over the stables. Gerald uses it as his den, bless him."

"Then I will get along there" Doctor said, standing up. Nurse held him back.

"Ten minutes. He'll be here. Guarantee it."

Again they sat in silence with more coffee. Then he heard it. A door banged down the corridor.

"This will be him now" Mrs Haveringham-Sim beamed. And at last the lounge door burst open, and Gerald made his magnificent entrance. He was all sweetness and light. His depression and the doll were seemingly forgotten. As soon as he saw the Doctor he rushed over to meet a new friend. His enthusiasm was so overwhelming that Doctor couldn't help liking the fellow. Even when he jumped upon his lap and licked his balding head!

Gerald was the largest, daftest and most loving black Labrador he had ever met.

For the rest of that month Gerald Haveringham-Sim was a constant companion on Doctor's visits. Whatever the problem had been, it was now solved.

When the Doctor came to leave that lovely part of the country and Gerald, it was like saying goodbye to a much loved child. He did promise to return as soon as possible to see Gerald again. But from the doleful expression upon his face he feared that very shortly Nurse Mort would be summoned once again to the Grange, this time to try and coax him out of his depression.

On reflection it was a sobering thought that Doctor was in the eyes of at least one devoted patient, more important than a rag doll!

1950 – Penny's Taster

The surgery door tentatively opened and a diminutive figure, clutching a home-made skipping rope appeared. She was skinny, brown as a berry with a mop of dark curly hair and hazel eyes. From behind his desk the doctor put her age at about eight years old, yet she appeared to be on her own, unusual for a child patient. Then he had a lot to learn about Cornish folk in the village to which he had come, initially as a locum.

"Hullo," he said, smiling. "Come along in and tell me who you are. And what the trouble is."

She fairly scampered across the room and stood before the desk as if she were standing in front of her school teacher. She pushed a slip of paper towards him, then stared down at her sockless feet in their scuffed, brown sandals.

The note was written in a round, neat hand and read quite simply, 'Penny has trouble with her water-works. Thank-you for seeing her.' It was signed 'Mrs Penrose,' presumably her mother.

"Couldn't Mummy come with you?" He asked gently. She shook her head, still looking down at her feet.

"So you are quite alone Penny?" The head suddenly lifted.

"No, Granddad is outside, waiting." A big smile lit up that little face; a smile that showed two missing front teeth and a sparkle in her hazel eyes.

"Should we call Granddad in? It would be best if he were here." Penny looked a bit crestfallen.

"I thought I was big coming on my own."

"And so you are sweetheart, but I still need to talk to a grown up if I have to give you any medicine."

Granddad turned out to be quite a youngish chap, whom Penny strongly resembled. He said he hadn't liked to intrude on the consultation, despite the child's age. He sat in the patient's chair while Penny came round to the doctor's side of the desk and whispered answers to his equally discreet questions. She giggled every so often. Giggled about her 'water works.' It was rather rude! But she didn't clam up with embarrassment.

The doctor told Granddad that he would need a sample of Penny's water before she started on any medicine. More giggles! And to the doctor's surprise Granddad turned a shade of red saying that a note had better be written about that to 'Mother'. It was.

The locum doctor was getting quite adept at concocting all sorts of mixtures in this dispensing practice. It was an art form, and patients liked to go away clutching their 'bottle'. The paediatric mixture for Penny would have to be 'potassium citrate with belladonna', not a very pleasant tasting preparation despite the addition of raspberry flavoured syrup. He returned from the dispensary brandishing the corked bottle. Penny's little face lost its smile and she fairly grimaced.

"Nasty medicine!" she shrieked.

"Not really" the doctor re-assured.

"May I please?" broke in Granddad, holding out his big hand. And taking the bottle he removed the cork, sniffed it, and appeared to sip a sample. He grinned. Turning to the child Granddad pronounced without hesitation.

"It's a right good drop of stuff he has given you little maid." The gummy smile returned to Penny's face.

Thankfully within a few days the distressing problem cleared up. But in no time at all she was back- still clutching the skipping rope – and with a nasty earache. The poor little mite still managed a smile, if fighting back tears. Again it was Granddad who accompanied her.

At that time there was not much in the way of antibiotics that could be given to the child by mouth, nor did they work as fast as those today. The doctor did not wish to resort to an injection of penicillin. Not for this poppet, brave enough though she was. In the dispensary the doctor produced a bottle of 'sulphadimidine mixture for infants', again a mixture made more palatable by raspberry syrup. Once again Granddad pre-tasted it and claimed it to be acceptable. If Granddad said it was all right, it must be!

The doctor stayed on in the practice and so watched Penny grow from a skinny child to a gangly teenager, and into an attractive young woman. A few days after her twenty-first birthday she married a local farmer's son. And in the natural course of time the doctor happily told her she was going to become a mother. The smile, if now adult, had not changed much.

At last the great day came and Penny went into labour. On receiving the call from the midwife the doctor called at the farmhouse and found all eager to get on with things, but Penny was a bit anxious which was only natural.

Sitting by her bed was, of course, Granddad. A much older Granddad holding Penny's hand. Nurse was about to administer what then was still the midwives' favourite sedative for 'first stage nerves', the vile mixture of 'potassium bromide and chloral.' Penny's eyes turned to Granddad. The doctor tried not to laugh for he knew what was about to happen. Granddad held out a by now very arthritic hand and politely took the spoon from Nurse, swallowing the medicine himself! Nurse stood open-mouthed. Without batting an eyelid the old boy turned to Penny and said, as on the first day the doctor met them both,

"Tis a good drop of stuff little maid." Without question or complaint Penny took the second spoonful proffered by the nurse. Despite the foul mixture she still managed one of her special smiles for them all. From then on it was plain sailing.

Although Granddad left the room during the birth itself, he was the first to appear as Nurse bathed the new-born baby girl. His joy was over-whelming. After a minute of holding his great-granddaughter he spoke.

"Well then, best go to my shed and make a new skipping rope. She'll need a skipping rope will the little maid."

Then that is what Granddads and Great-Granddads are for. Apart from tasting medicine!

A HOME VISIT IN RURAL CORNWALL, 1960'S

1952 – Drinks and Nibbles

In his youth the doctor had often been subjected to helping out at cocktail or drinks parties at the homes of relatives, with lots of 'loud' friends. Then he was not old enough to join in the 'browsing and sluicing'. He, and any cousins of a similar age, were merely unpaid waiters with plates of crisps, nuts and delicacies on sticks – cocktail sausages, plus strange nibbles wrapped in bacon with rather fancy names such as an 'amused girl'. Bits and pieces to go with the gin or scotch. Yet it was these 'dos' that gave him an insight into the party banter and babble of well-irrigated folk from the professional classes – all talking at the same time!

What, you may be wondering, has all this got to do with matters medical? In itself really very little about clinical medicine, except the sight of the occasional General Practitioner guest being 'buttonholed' in one corner by a large lady demanding to know about the very latest slimming pills!

A dozen or so years later the doctor, working in hospital, went to many parties in 'the Residents quarters' – parties that often would degenerate into 'benders'. Yet, if the consultant staff gate-crashed some special occasion like a leaving 'do' (as they were wont to do) talk reverted to 'shop' or cases of interest up on the wards. (To the would-be doctor/writer all this was grist to his or her literary mill.) What follows is a 'tincture of an example'.

* * * *

The young housemen and women all placed bets on which Consultant would corner another specialist to discuss a topic of purely professional interest. Other bets were on who would not speak to whom, or if indeed fighting would break out! Parties in the Residents could get like that when the ale flowed, or the wine was taken too readily.

The hot money was on a particularly pompous Surgical Registrar, still young, but up-and-coming with a high opinion of his own ability, that while not inconsiderable, was not as yet polished enough for even greater office. He had once told an elderly patient with an obvious diagnosis of pancreatic cancer that it was "just a bit of nonsense that can be dealt with in an afternoon." The poor old boy had died within the week. There was a post mortem and the Surgical Reg. had the nerve to go to the mortuary and beg for the diseased organ to use as a teaching specimen. Thereafter every decent house surgeon tried to avoid referring cases to him on account of his blasé bedside manner and brusqueness with patients, especially the elderly. Yet he still strutted around like a peacock and was thought to be the first doctor in the hospital to be seen with his stethoscope draped round the back of his neck and along his shoulders as is done today with the lightweight Littman instruments....yet back to the party.

Sure enough the Registrar made a bee-line for the hospital's Senior Surgeon. Here was a wonderful, gentle man who largely specialised on the bladder. The blasted Surgical Reg. sidled up and said in a loud voice "John, do you still refer your haemorrhoid cases to old Brownlow?"

"Why so, Mr Barton?" the Chief asked with patience, then sipped a large whisky & soda. He continued quietly "Think I can still carry out a neat haemorrhoidectomy. However, I do agree Brownlow is still the very best man for proctology cases in this hospital. But what is the problem Barton? Thrombosed are they? Or are you having a bit of 'botty bother' yourself at the moment?" A rhetorical question, for answer there came none! It was a wonderful put down. And Barton made an embarrassed excuse that his call lights were 'up', thus beating a hasty retreat.

Another surgeon who could not but hear the conversation remarked to the Chief "You know Jack, Barton is a most trying young man! But talking of John Brownlow, he was wonderful during the war you recall. Led the hospital teams through the most dire of times and never batted an eyelid. Worked hour after hour when we had our bit of a Blitz." Other voices agreed, coming in with their own memories. The young doctor thought of the man in question. New House Officers feared being 'bellowed at' but none had a bad word for him. He did not stand for laziness, nor pandered to busy-body Administrators. And he never failed to stand up for HIS lads and lasses if they were 'on the carpet' for anything remotely serious.

"How is the fishing Paddy?" asked a florid faced gynaecologist of a cardiologist colleague, who was a quiet reserved man who had just dropped into the party out of courtesy.

"Very good.....in Ireland." Came the reply. "I'm going over again next week."

The gynaecologist merely beamed and then grumbled "The only thing I will be fishing for next week will be cervical polypi, or the odd Bartholin's cyst. I say, these vol-au-vent things look tempting. What's in them? Oh, mushrooms, jolly good!"

The best thing a shy doctor could do at these parties, until of course he or she got a few drinks down, was to loiter on the edge or strike up a conversation – preferably not 'shop' with immediate contemporaries. Yet it soon happened that the most feared surgeon or physician who had told you off that morning, tended to soon forget the matter and chat away in a matey manner, even to the extent of hinting that he had a place for a new S.H.O coming up and if one was interested, well a good word would be put in the appropriate ear.

Many of these 'drinks and nibbles' parties were just for the doctors, and many of the nurses of course, to relax if off-duty, or grab a bun and a weak 'snifter' if on-duty and briefly away from the ward or Casualty. The call lights would catch you wherever you were. However, this 'do' was indeed a real celebration, hence the number of consultants arriving with welcome bottles of spirits not usually affordable by the junior staff.

This was rather special. One of the 'high-flying' Medical Registrars had become an M.D. which also coincided with his appointment as a 'Fellow' of the Royal College of Physicians. We were all proud and pleased for Andrew, who was the best of chaps as well as an outstanding doctor.

We all knew that one of the cardiologists was contemplating retirement so maybe Andrew would quickly be offered a Consultancy here, but the usual way of doing things was to rise to these dizzy heights at a hospital in London or one of the other large cities where the major hospital had its own medical school, or if one was lucky see what was on offer at one's own teaching hospital.

Meanwhile the chatting had risen and a variety of discussions were in progress.

"Of course he always has been red-hot on liver disease" observed a passing pathologist on the way to the whisky.

"I saw a rather interesting liver the other day" another pathologist broke in. "You should have seen the hob-nails on the thing. Classic!"

"Was that the old soak on '2 top' ward?" a female surgical officer asked, coming up with a gin & tonic, just replenished, and a glint in her eye.

"Ah Cecily" grunted the pathologist. "Did you get my full report?"

"I haven't seen it yet. There seems to be some sort of hiatus in the path.admin office."

"Well dear" boomed the pathologist, drinking deeply of his whisky, "it was the best of its kind I have seen since the war in the Middle East. I will certainly 'bottle' that liver for future reference"

"I will look forward to reading the full story." Cecily replied. "Perhaps 'old soak' was a bit harsh - I rather took to her. Hardly thought she was a heavy drinker."

"No more than any of us, eh?" laughed the other.

After thirty minutes more of medical banter, and a wink from a blonde Ward Sister, all hell broke loose for the young doctor. All four call lights began flashing manically. The Sister came to him and murmured something about waiting for him in Cas. Sister's sitting room. As he pulled on his white coat which was to hand, a pal remarked that being a Casualty Officer was a sod, and leered at the blonde Sister. Before dashing away he sought out Andrew and wished him 'God speed' yet quietly arranged to meet him in the local pub tomorrow, before he left.

The case urgently awaiting him in Casualty was a young man with a severe attack of asthma. He had been placed on the examination couch stripped to the waist and supported by pillows. His breathing was rattling, but as he fought to breathe out it took a long time to get through the tiny tubes in his lungs due to constriction and sticky sputum which was also caking his bluish lips. His radial pulses raced at 145 beats per minute. From a thick wad of past Cas. Cards, the doctor found him to be a regular visitor to the Department, who responded well to adrenaline 1:1000 given slowly, intravenously, but had recently been given a new drug called isoprenaline, by the Senior Medical Registrar. As this had worked, the young doctor decided with the SMR's blessing to prescribe this drug again, and also have a word with the patient's own doctor. Asking for the SMR's lights to go up, he waited for the phone to ring. When it did, from the noise in the background he knew where his Chief was. The party. After all was done for the asthmatic and the medical emergency abated, he wondered if it was worth going back to the party. Then he remembered his girl-friend, presumably still in Sister's sitting room.

* * * *

His understanding friend had left a message with Staff Nurse to say she had returned to the party. The doctor had a cup of coffee, kindly offered in Cas., and changed into a clean white coat not splattered with sticky sputum. Before he could get back to the internal doors of the 'Residents' up went his lights. Again!

For a brief moment he felt it would have been preferable if he was back in his teens, handing round to long-gone, pipe-smoking, Lloyds banking, Uncles, with their whisky & sodas and laughing Aunts, tiddley on their third G&T; all those nibbles, but in a comfortable lounge with a roaring fire in the grate. And of course, NO BLASTED COLOURED LIGHTS ON THE WALL.

1958 – Four Coloured Lights… Flashing

Friday 22nd August 1958. 9:45pm

Sixteen year old Hilary Johnstone was in her bedroom/study preparing for her O-level exams. Her grey eyes were tired. Running a hand through her bobbed blond hair, she decided enough was done for one evening. Three hours of biology, physics and chemistry had left her head spinning.

Being a Friday evening, father was out. Mother was taking a restful bath. Hilary walked down the narrow landing to call through the door of the bathroom to ask if her mother wanted a milky drink when she got into bed. She tapped on the door; then instinctively knew something was wrong. There were sounds of noisy breathing coming from mother, mixed with marked pauses. Hilary cried out and banged on the stout door. There was no response. She must get in. A sturdy girl, Hilary placed her back against the opposite wall and gave the locked door a heavy kick. It shuddered, then a second kick did the trick and the door sprung open. Mother was lying in an empty bath, hanging over the side and deeply unconscious. She had also vomited. The doctor must be urgently called, and Hilary rushed to the telephone in the hall downstairs.

Dr Eva McKinnon promptly answered her phone. Hilary kept cool and gave a quick and exact summary of mother's condition. The doctor knew Hilary well and trusted her observations. She said "Good girl Hilary. Keep calm dear. Leave the front door open for me – I'm on my way."

As Hilary replaced the telephone receiver, the front door opened and thankfully father came in. One look at his daughter's frightened face told him something was terribly wrong. They both managed to get the wet body of mother completely out of the bath and on to the floor. This coincided with a voice from the landing, and Eva McKinnon came in with her small medical case. She was quickly bending over the limp form making a swift assessment of the patient. (She suspected a 'stroke' from what Hilary had said on the phone. She now feared the worst.)

Dr McKinnon put a comforting arm round Hilary's shoulders, saying "This girl did everything calmly and correctly. Now Hilary, slip on your coat and go to the front gate. The ambulance won't be long coming, then you can show the crew where your mother is." The doctor was by now down in the hall and picking up the telephone receiver dialling '999'.

Hilary did as she was asked but had the courage to refrain from asking the obvious question..."Will mother die?"

The cold misty air and damp leaves of that suburban road caused the girl to shiver. She also felt a bit sick. Maybe she was in shock, so leaned against a tree. Very soon the headlights of a blue/grey ambulance, its bell giving a short burst, turned from the main road and as Hilary waved it down, pulled up beside the kerb. Two very calm men in white coats and peaked caps came to her, one placing a large hand on her shaking shoulders. His action slowed the garbled story. "Easy now lovey. We'll take it from here. Patient upstairs is she?"

"Yes. The doctor and my father are with her."

"Is it your mother who is the patient?" the driver gently asked.

"Yes. I heard strange breathing from the bathroom. She was hanging over the side of an empty bath. Unconscious." The tears suddenly welled up, but the ambulance crew were quick to comfort Hilary.

"Try not to get too upset love. Show us where she is, and we will soon have her up to the General Hospital. If the doctor has also rung Casualty then they will be expecting her."

The rear doors of the ambulance were opened, and a stretcher, plus a carrying sheet were brought into the hall. Only this latter was taken up the winding staircase. Dr McKinnon knew the ambulance driver and called him Ken. She had a few quiet words with the crew and as she wrote a short note to the Casualty Officer, skilled hands placed Mrs Johnstone onto the waiting stretcher. Father had gently covered his wife's naked body with his dressing gown where it remained, but was covered with a further grey ambulance blanket.

As Mr Johnstone had no car the doctor got him and Hilary into her car. They followed the ambulance up to the hospital. By the time they climbed Park Row and turned left through the gates into the courtyard, the ambulance was already backed up to the open glass doors of the ambulance bay.

Hilary was overwhelmed by all the bright lights, broken only by a vertical strip of coloured lights – green at the top, then red, orange and white at the base. They all flashed together. They were the doctor's 'call lights'.

The stretcher bearing Mrs Johnstone now rested on a trolley chassis, and the ambulance crew were joined in the entrance corridor by Night Sister, unflustered and immaculate in her dark blue uniform and frilly cap which was neatly tied under her chin. The flashing lights stopped as a white coated doctor appeared and followed the trolley into one of the two emergency examination rooms. He paused at the curtained entrance and had a few words with Dr McKinnon, who passed him her note. Before Sister followed the group she showed Mr Johnstone and a frightened Hilary to the semi-gloom of the Casualty waiting area with its hard polished benches.

Dr McKinnon came and said goodbye and offered comfort. As she turned to leave she gave Hilary a little hug. "Be brave dear" she said. Father thanked her for all her kindness, then the Sister appeared and took him and Hilary to speak to the young Casualty Officer. The ambulance crew were still here and had been asked to wheel the trolley down to the ward taking medical cases that evening. A red blanket now covered mother. The doctor looked grave. He told them it was clearly a serious stroke, but as to the outcome – the House Physician would have a better idea of that after a full examination and tests on the ward. She was being admitted under the Consultant Dr Dennis Porter. Dr Porter tended to appear at the hospital just before midnight to see what cases had come in, and generally back up his exhausted junior staff. Hilary and her father caught up with the trolley as it reached the lift down to the women's medical ward W.G.2.

A pretty staff nurse showed Hilary and her father to a side room just round a corner from the ward doors. Cups of strong tea were produced and welcome.

After about half an hour the door opened and another Night Sister, together with a young doctor, came in. Hilary suddenly blurted out "Has my mother died? Oh no!" Sister laid a hand on her arm. "No, no. She is very ill I'm afraid."

The doctor cleared his throat and tended to fiddle with the chest-piece of his stethoscope. He admitted he was 'rather new to medicine' but understood that even patients with severe cerebral haemorrhages could often make a good recovery. Sister tended to back him up.

They were told they could stay as long as they liked. Perhaps Hilary would like to go for a walk, even get some air in the court-yard. "If you get lost just ask a member of staff to direct you back to ward W.G.2." On her stroll she saw the Casualty Officer sitting on a low wall smoking his pipe. Hilary smiled at him. He was younger than she had first thought. They had a pleasant little chat, then he caught sight of the 4 flashing coloured lights which coincided with an ambulance coming through the gates and 'backing up' to the glass doors.

"Here we go again" the doctor grinned. "For heaven's sake don't be a doctor when you choose what to do in later life."

Back in the waiting room, father put an arm round his only child and said "I've been through all this before you know." Hilary kissed him.

Mother died at noon the following day.

* * * *

1964. September.

A newly qualified, pre-Registration House Physician sat writing up the case notes of an elderly lady she had just admitted and examined. There was much to record. The case notes folder was thick and had been written in by doctors from many specialities going back several years.

The problems were mostly medical – except for a partial gastrectomy five years back – to try and clear a recurrent stomach ulcer that would not respond to conventional medicine. The new girl on the block wondered if she should ask her very approachable Consultant Physician whether, due to this latest crop of problems, the patient should be referred back to Mr Shaw the Senior Surgeon, who had done the operation?

As the doctor pondered a moment, she glanced up and spotted the single green light flashing on the call lights over the ward doors. It was her light, and this was actually the first time she had need to answer it. Picking up the telephone receiver she tried to sound confident. "Doctor Johnstone. You have my lights up?"

She was requested by the Casualty Officer to come and take a look at a collapse just in. The young Indian doctor on the phone sounded as nervous as Hilary Johnstone felt.

1992. Nottingham: An afternoon in late spring.

On a late Spring afternoon in 1992 an attractive middle-aged lady strolled through Nottingham's Park Valley, a residential gem of large houses and their magnificent well-established gardens. She savoured the area, knowing it well. Her intention was to eventually reach and climb a set of worn and winding steps that would bring her up to the gate of the General Hospital where the buildings overlooked some of the most desirable addresses in the city.

The climb was not as easy as she had known it in her youth. And the hospital had changed; not for the better. It was of course coming to the end of its useful days and only partially open. However, this former House Officer hoped whoever was in charge would allow her to stroll round what remained of her youthful memories, but it was a bit like going back to a much loved school. There would be frightful disappointments she was sure.

At the top of the flight of steps there was still the old green gate into the back garden of what had been known as Broxtowe House, the 'Residents' accommodation. Hilary Johnstone, for that was the lady doctor's name, had her room here 28 years ago. What happiness she had shared here. Hard work and worry over patients, but fun too. The house looked all but abandoned. Maybe what resident staff were still in charge had all transferred to a second house on the Ropewalk, which had also been in use all those years ago.

She stood outside the hospital gates and got her bearings.

* * * *

If Hillary looked to her right she could see down Park Row into the town, but looking straight ahead out of the gate the view was directly along the Ropewalk, past the Pay Bed Block on one side and on the other, Out-patients, above which was the Ear, Nose and Throat Department; and above that the Radio-Therapy ward and administrative offices. Behind the left-hand side of the Ropewalk from this spot ran Park Terrace and the 'rooms' of various Consultants.

Hilary Johnstone turned and walked through the still-open gates, across the courtyard and up to the main entrance. She hoped to find someone in charge still and get permission to have a last look round. She could see behind the old buildings the large Trent Wing that had only started 'rising' just before she had left the Hospital in the 60s. Where this was erected had once been tennis courts and a garden, where patients 'on the mend' could sit out during good weather to watch the doctors and nurses enjoy their fun.

Hilary's reverie was broken by the strident tones of a lady obviously 'in charge'. "And just where do you think you are going?" It was like being back at school. She turned to see a grey haired woman with a sallow face and cross expression. 'Dr Johnstone' explained who she was and asked if 'as an old member of staff' she could fulfil her wish of one last look round. The other party's tone mellowed, and she said that there was not now much of the old 'interior' to see. Most of the remaining patients were in the Trent Wing, what wards remained in this part of the hospital were closed and padlocked for safety's sake. However, Dr Johnstone could wander round if she was careful. Hilary thanked the woman – to a departing back!

Coming through the Main Entrance she noticed the Head Porter's Office on the right was now used for storage, while a little office on the left seemed still in use, although for now it was empty. It had been here that Hilary had filled in her first death certificate when becoming a Senior House Officer.

Coming into the vestibule with its small waiting area, Hilary was in a short corridor she knew well. If she turned left she would come to the entrance of the male accident ward. Beside this was a flight of steps leading to the male surgical ward on the floor above. She turned right and passed a few two-or-three bedded wards for any overspill of orthopaedic, then headed down the slightly sloping corridor, to face the ground floor ward of the notable 'rotunda' Jubilee Wing that comprised four fine surgical wards – the main surgical wing of the hospital. Gingerly she walked up this to the first ward where she had done her pre-registration surgery job. The doors of this well-known ward were chained and padlocked and bore red notices 'shouting' UNSAFE. It was a sad sight. A man's voice was heard calling to her "You won't find any patients up here young lady!" Turning, she looked down the steps to see a chap of 'sixtyish'. He wore theatre scrubs. A surgeon of the old times, or perhaps a porter. Hilary descended to his side. He wore the now obligatory name badge. It read 'Dr N. J. Lane – Anaesthetist'. His face was vaguely familiar from long past, yet not from her time there. Further back still. He went on "I sense you are on a nostalgic visit. The old place has gone to seed a bit, bless it. I too am back after a long spell away."

Hilary smiled and offered her hand. "I'm pleased to meet you Dr Lane. I am Hilary Johnstone." They warmly shook hands. Still his face seemed in some way familiar. Little did she know that he too was struggling in a similar manner.

"I did my pre-registration year here back in 1964. Then after that I was lucky enough to get a Casualty S.H.O. post for another year." Nick Lane laughed and gave his résumé. "Well, back in the 1950s I too did my pre-reg stint here. Indeed, going round and round this bally Jubilee Wing. Then on to Portland Ward and six months medicine." Hilary grinned and he thought she looked so very young. She would have been a real 'smasher' as a girl. He had a good memory for faces if not names.

"May I ask did you ever come to the hospital before 1964? I mean I didn't have the pleasure of taking out your appendix or anything like that?"

"No kind sir" Hilary laughed. "I would have remembered you in that delightful connection I'm sure." Then it struck her! She asked quietly "I know you cannot possibly remember every patient you saw, but did you ever cover in Casualty in your surgical or medical months?"

He thought, and a memory came to him. "During the summer of '58 we had a bit of a problem with Casualty Officers, especially at night. I certainly gave a hand then. It brought in a few more 'bob'. Yes, there was one teenage girl. Came in late one night. I think – and it is a very vague think – but the patient was her mother. A known hypertension who had a massive cerebral haemorrhage." Hilary completed the memory…."and you later sat outside on the courtyard wall smoking your pipe and chatted to her."

"Good gracious yes. I think I told her never to become a doctor."

"Well she didn't take any notice!"

"And what exactly did you do after leaving this 'charnel house'? he grinned, continuing, "Sorry, I'm a bit of a blighter for getting an accurate history – force of habit and all that." Of course Hilary didn't mind. As doctors they had certain ingrown habits. They were both of a kind, despite the age difference, which was not that much.

"In 1967 I decided to take up General Practice locally. And of course there was my father to consider. He was retired but still living in the family home."

"Is your father…" he stopped. "Sorry, daft question."

"Dead. Yes poor old pa never lived to see me qualify. Died in his sleep in 1962. He never really got over mother. Life didn't give him much of a hand. Spent all his money on my education." She looked momentarily sad.

"Did you like family medicine?" Nick changed the subject.

"In the early years yes, but now with all the changes it's a bit bloody. And it looks like getting worse. Another day, another directive from our blasted unqualified masters. I am only working part-time now. I also do a bit of paediatric casualty at the Queens."

"Still like getting vomit on your shoes?" They both laughed. Nick had realised that she had said nothing about being married. She wore no ring. Hilary was thinking the same thing at the same time! She did brazenly ask "Have you any family Nick?"

"I fear…" he tried to look serious…"I'm a bit of a failure in the matrimonial stakes. I was engaged twice, then married, but the lady in question soon ran away to foreign climes. If you'll pardon the expression, it was all a bit of a 'bugger' really.

"And work kept you sane?"

"With that lot behind me I needed the money. Will you trust me to buy you tea?"

Just before they walked back down the Jubilee Wing steps, Hilary asked Nick "Can one still get into Shipstone Theatre?"

He smiled "I'm glad you asked that. Indeed it is the very reason our paths have met. It is still accessible and I want to see if there is an original 'quick-acting' Mason mouth gag in there."

Up they went again to the corridor above, off which was the operating theatre. While still un-locked, it was clearly 'moth-balled' – a dumping place for obsolete equipment of all kinds. Everything had been disconnected. Instruments were scattered on the floor. Hilary still remembered it well. The hiss of sterilizers; the smell of the anaesthetics of her day. A few spare or empty cylinders of oxygen, nitrous oxide, carbon dioxide/oxygen and cyclopropane were propped up in one corner, beside which was an old 'Boyles' anaesthetic apparatus. Nick gave a hoot of joy and rumbled around in one of the drawers between the working surface with all the flow-meters for the ether and chloroform, plus the attached cylinders. Also the long breathing tubes and various sizes of mask were to hand at one side. "Got one!" Nick said gleefully, taking the shiny 'gag' from the drawer. "Just the job. What a bloody waste of good sound workable equipment." He smiled across at Hilary who was fondling a retractor. "Happy memories, eh Miss Johnstone? Did one of the long gone surgical chiefs throw that at you sometime?"

Hilary grinned back. "No, but I often got lumbered with hanging on to this or one of its pals."

With a head full of memories Hilary walked with Nick Lane down to the Main corridor, which once accommodated the administrative offices, and more fearful still, Matron's room; but now no scared nurses stood in a line outside the heavy door.

The café on the ground floor of the Trent Wing had its doors open onto the corridor just past what had been Matron's den. Nick looked in and turned to Hilary, pulling a face.

"It all looks packed and noisy in there" he said. "Come on 'ducky' I have a better idea if you like it." He suddenly gently took Hilary's arm and led her on down the endless corridor. They came to an elbow bend by the doors of another closed and dark ward.

"Good Lord!" exclaimed Hilary "University Ward. Old dears with fractured femurs…and ever the smell of pee and cabbage."

Nick laughed out loud. "Give that girl a coconut! Come on, we're nearly there." "Surely you're not taking me into our dear old home? Broxtowe House? I thought from the outside it was empty and unused?"

He led her to the right, down a short flight of steps and into the Resident's quarters. It had hardly changed.

"A few of us still have rooms here. And the rest room has tea-making facilities still – so there my girl"

It all seemed very much as it had in her day, which pleased Hilary no end.

"Pardon me for asking Nick" she continued, "but is the loo still in the same place? Tiddley-wee time. Must be getting old." She laughed. A typically attractive, girlish laugh. She did suddenly feel very happy.

"If Madam would care to step this way…" Nick opened another door and pointed down a short passage. "On the right. Surely you remember the 'throne room' we all loved?"

She opened the door and gasped "My God I can't believe it" A large convenience with a very ornate lavatory on an ornate marble slab, with behind it a stained glass window almost smiled down at her. It had been a gift from a wealthy patient in toilet-fittings!

Coming back to the rest room Hilary was still amused, even joyous, at seeing something so memorable from her past. She curled up on a battered sofa, accepting the cup of tea Nick had made for her, and laid on a tray.

"I don't think this room has changed very much since I left in early '66. In fact I'm sure it hasn't. That pile of medical journals look the same, only further up the wall! She broke into giggles. Nick decided to play along with her, or was it mild flirting?

"I think they have emptied the big ash-trays once or twice. And my dear old pipe is missing." So they chatted on. It would seem that Nick Lane had returned to London in '61 to study anaesthetics with the view of getting a senior post in the speciality. He had a go, but Consultantships were difficult to come by so he too had gone back to Casualty work, taking a SHO post in Birmingham, about the time Hilary was settling down in suburban general practice in Nottingham. In the late '70s several Nottingham anaesthetists retired and with the coming of the new Teaching Hospital a grand new Department emerged and Nick had got his foot in the door. He gave cover in various out-flung smaller hospitals in the County. He was now on the road to retirement, but still – until final closure – would do work at the General, Trent Wing theatres.

He realised he had waffled on a bit, but Hilary now felt she had known him for years. In a way, she had. He glanced at his watch.

"Have you got to get back for an evening surgery?" he asked.

"Do you want to hustle me out?" Hilary teased.

"Lord no. I have a bit more nostalgia for you, if you haven't had enough."

"Dr Lane I am totally free for the rest of today. I came here to lay a ghost or two, and wish the old place a fond goodbye. It is a sad prospect now, yet I think something could have been done with it. A geriatric hospital or, since two fine psychiatric hospitals are but posh housing for the wealthy, this would have been helpful to the community.

"They are not 'politically correct' of course. The politicians believe in freedom from helpful and often necessary restraint – God help us. It's the same all over the land, Hilary love." Nick suddenly wondered if he'd been too outspoken; "I apologise for my familiarity".

"Apologies are unnecessary Nick. I don't take offence at being called 'love', 'me Duck', 'sweetheart'. Why get worked up over terms of endearment, unless they are perhaps given with a leer." She laughed "And you do not leer."

Nick looked hard at her then said "Cor! Hee, k-woo!"

"Now, dear heart, you are just being daft. I bet you were always daft, and a real Romeo when a student."

"Oh yes" he said "Come back to my digs and see my skeleton sometime. I don't like pretending to be a 'dapper' old rake now life is getting on. And I haven't asked you if you have a husband and children to go home to."

His question out of the blue, had Hilary taken a little aback. "I have been married."

"Another doctor, may I ask?" said Nick.

"No, a lovely policeman actually. I met him in Casualty, but he died a year later. A rather sudden and fast ca. pancreas. I've been bloody unlucky with men." There was a pause, neither knowing how to continue. Hilary again broke the silence.

"Have dinner with me at the George this evening. If you are not on call to gas people that is."

Nick came and took her hands "Very much as old friends?"

"Of course. I'm not, as you remember girls saying…fast!"

"I do have one more surprise for you Hilary." Nick walked over and drew back a dusty curtain. There on the wall was an old strip of 'call lights'. He reached for a switch and the whole lot started flashing…green at the top, then red; orange and white at the base.

"How on earth..!" Hilary exclaimed.

"I got one of the old electricians to set this up in here. It was due for the scrap heap. Several of us older doctors wanted at least one memory of the pre-bleep age. Works from a switch for each light and a continuous one for all to go at once: what do you think?"

Hilary thought back 34 years to a group of people, a trolley outside what had been room 1, and a frightened girl; then the arrival of a good looking young Casualty Officer. She took from her handbag a battered buff Casualty card – pinched when she was on the staff here. Pinched before the old notes were destroyed. She handed it to Nick.

"Think you will recognise the writing Nick my dear." Reading it, he looked up at Hilary. "A sad but worthy memento."

The card and attached G.P's note told the story…and more:

'Known hypertension, age 56, found collapsed in bathroom this evening. Deeply comatose. Pin-point pupils. Cheyne-Stokes breathing. Increased jerks. Left hemiplegia. ADMIT MED. TAKE. ? C.V.A.

The lights stopped flashing, so hand in hand they crept away – giggling!

* * * *

Footnote: In later years I got to know many Doctor's at this hospital, plus ambulance crews and Officers. I was working in the Casualty Department in the early 1960's.

To those still alive I send best wishes.

To those – and there are many – now departed – **May they Rest in Peace**.

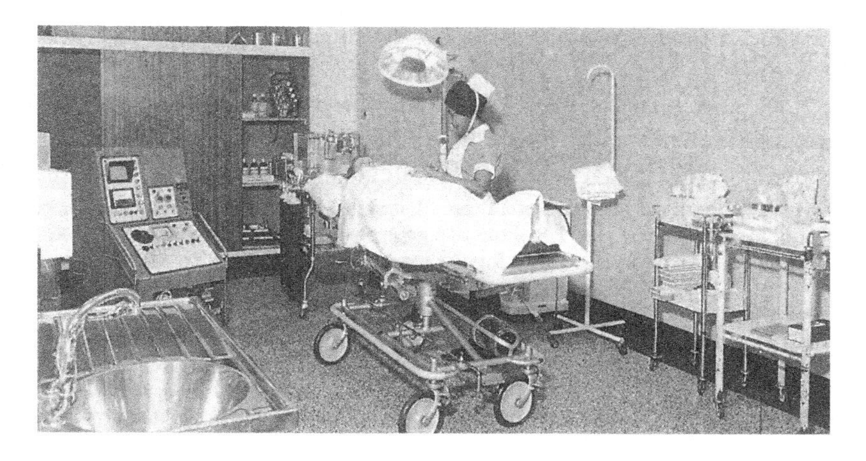

CASUALTY DEPARTMENT DRESSINGS ROOM, 1960

1958 – Soft Soap and Castor Oil

The wet summer of 1958 did not deter the increasing number of holiday-makers coming to Portherack on the Cornish peninsula. These folk and the growing resident population brought extra work for Dr Walter Welbeloved, thirty years the village general practitioner.

At this time one of his regular functions was to attend all home confinements. Usually he just observed, made noises of encouragement and performed any fancy needlework required thereafter. It was 'Nurse' who conducted the main event. It was the heyday of the district nurse/midwife, in this location a task performed by two admirable ladies, Nurses Rush and Tuggitt. And from the midwifery aspect both were equally competent and well liked, apart of course from their fervent belief in the value of castor oil and soft soap enemas to get things going!

By an amazing historical co-incidence both ladies had come to the area within weeks of each other in 1948. Equally coincidental was the fact that by this wet August some years later, both had attended ninety-seven births each. Up until the end of the year there were booked five more confinements spread over the district. The race for the hundredth baby was on.

As each nurse/midwife covered for the other, there was an element of luck-of-the-draw. Either could have three straight births in a row. But if things went on an alternate basis for the next four confinements, the fifth arrival would decide the winner. Looking at all the due dates by 'batting order' baby number five would be born to Mrs Trevose of Portherack, and was lined up for Christmas Day, which would make it extra special for Muriel Tuggitt with whom she was officially booked.

In this challenging scenario the geographical aspects of the area would play a great part. While they worked mainly for Dr Welbeloved out of the Portherack surgery, Nurse Tuggitt came from Tregissey, four miles to the West and the Lizard Point, while Nurse Rush lived six miles to the North East, near the

Helford Estuary in 'Frenchman's Creek' country. Both cared for a large number of patients, including those on the list of a Dr Smiley. He in turn covered for Welbeloved on a flexible rota system. All were happy with the set-up. Yet Nurse Rush did have one advantage over Nurse Tuggitt in that she owned a small motor car. Nurse Tuggitt remained firmly attached to her bicycle; she could cheerfully pedal many a mile with amazing speed and ease, even when loaded with nursing bags, the gas-and-air apparatus and other equipment.

September came and went, and in mellow October, when Cornish hedges are heavy with blackberries, Muriel Tuggitt gained an advantage. If she had a fault, Nurse Rush was inclined to live up to her name and dash everywhere in a 'scatty' manner. One morning when visiting an old man near Helford, she saw to his ablutions then sat him on the commode while she made them a cup of tea. When she was done, in her hurry to get him back to bed, she made the fatal mistake of neglecting her proper back positioning. Her back 'went'. In great pain she had completed her rounds and evening surgery saw her on Dr Smiley's couch being moved this way and that, and rapped with his percussor. Fortunately there was no slipped disc, but a period of bed rest, warmth and codeine compound tablets was required.

In the fourteen days Mary Rush was laid-up Nurse Tuggitt brought two of the five babies into the world. She had now delivered her ninety-ninth. The century was in sight. Yet the all-important Christmas baby was still nearly two months off, and with two babies due before it, chances were that she might well get her century but Nurse Rush would enjoy the kudos of the Christmas birth.

A November night saw Nurse Tuggitt cycling fast along a winding lane. In the pitch-black she was unable to see the wet cow-pat ahead of her, and as the front wheel slid through it the bike went over and Nurse was hurled into the ditch. Muriel Tuggitt was shaken but found the only damage to herself was a grazed shin. The bike fared worse. Its front wheel was twisted and the forks splayed, but as the expectant mother to whom she was going needed attention sooner than herself or the bike, she had to find a telephone box and ask Nurse Rush to stand in for her. The request was met with a willingness that indicated the competition was still on! Within the hour Nurse Rush had delivered a healthy baby boy at Garwarren. Then, early the following morning she was called to the sudden delivery of another baby on Nurse Tuggitt's list. They were ninety-nine all!

With no other confinements due except Mrs Trevose, Muriel Tuggitt and Mary Rush busied themselves with the district nursing side of their work.

Winter produced many folk who by rights should have gone into hospital, yet insisted on staying put in their own beds to enjoy the devotion of doctors and nurses they knew and trusted. So, Christmas Day approached. Reliable 'mum' that she was, Mrs Trevose started the first stage of labour early on the afternoon of Christmas Eve. She called Nurse Tuggitt who appeared very soon and confirmed that things were definitely 'go'. Nurse then left, promising to return at 7.00pm prompt to administer the soft soap enema. Thankfully there was no hint that the castor oil would be required this time.

Just after she had pedalled away, who should arrive in her car but Nurse Rush, having been told of the situation as a matter of routine. There were more smiles and words of encouragement for Mrs Trevose, and offering the season's greetings Nurse Rush too went on her way, but not before leaving note of all the places she could be contacted if things did suddenly speed up, and Nurse Tuggitt had not got back on time.

Mrs Trevose watched the little car roar off, not caring a hoot who delivered her. All she wanted was to get the turkey stuffed, fill the children's stockings and make sure the place was tidy in time for the arrival of her mother-in-law from Helston. And then she had to satisfy a craving for a slice of pork pie and some pickled onions.

At seven o'clock on the dot Nurse Tuggitt arrived back in Portherack with all her gear for the delivery. Everything was going nicely to plan and after the enema she estimated that Mrs

Trevose would give birth around one o'clock on Christmas morning. Nurse Tuggitt couldn't stay with her because she had some other visits to fit in that evening, but she promised faithfully to return just before midnight.

Heading out towards Goonhilly Downs, Nurse Tuggitt bore gifts for an old lady for whom she had long cared. She wanted to see this patient was not in any pain from her arthritis and resting peacefully. This was certainly so – she was dead!

This situation placed Nurse Tuggitt in a dreadful fix. Fortunately the cottage had recently had a telephone installed. Dr Smiley, who was on duty, had to be called, and Nurse Rush asked to be on standby for Mrs Trevose, just in case Nurse Tuggitt could not do all that was necessary and get back to Portherack for midnight.

The doctor was in, but Nurse Rush had gone to visit friends prior to attending midnight mass at the little church in her home village of St. Julien. Her husband said he would try and contact her and send her to Portherack.

Nurse Tuggitt awaited Dr Smiley and the local police constable. This was a sudden death so the Coroner's Office had to be informed. The doctor and the policeman arrived together within half an hour, carried out their respective tasks and left Nurse to prepare the body for the undertaker to remove for post mortem at Portherack Cottage Hospital.

Given a clear road and with fast pedalling, Nurse Tuggitt broke all her previous records and arrived breathless at Mrs Trevose's cottage just before twelve-thirty. She expected to find Nurse Rush already weighing her hundredth baby. Not so, for Nurse Rush's car lights suddenly appeared round the corner. They met at the gate.

"Your mother. Your baby, Nurse" Mary Rush smiled.

"Thank you Nurse" Muriel Tuggitt replied politely, then continued, "Should we make it a joint effort? What do you say?"

"Splendid idea" Mary Rush beamed. They rang the bell.

Mr Trevose answered the door wearing a paper hat and holding a pint of Devenish. He appeared distinctly merry. "Come in my hansoms" he welcomed. "Join the party."

Both nurses looked amazed. In the brightly lit cottage a merry throng greeted them, including Dr Welbeloved, all smiles, with a new-born baby in his arms

"Ah, dear ladies" he exclaimed. "I'm happy to say this one is mine, and its years since I brought a Christmas baby into the world. What a truly happy event."

The nurses were speechless. Then the joy of the occasion dispelled all personal disappointment. And the race for the hundredth was still to be won!

Postscript: previously published in several medical magazines.

1960 – Drama due to Max and Ben

Christmas Day

Back in the days when family doctors were willing to take turns with the practice 'partners' to take calls over Christmas and Bank Holidays, it often seemed to happen that a cry for help was made just as the doctor and his family were about to sit down to lunch, or try to relax a while. What follows is an example.

Dr Fellows had, fortunately, only risked a small aperitif with his wife, as the children were opening their presents just before Christmas lunch.

When he came back from the phone in the passage beyond the dining room, his wife looked mildly annoyed. "Can it wait a bit?" she asked hopefully. The doctor shook his head. "I think not, from the racket in the background. I could get no real sense from the caller, and there is some sort of injury I believe. I had best go, and 'grumble at them' afterwards if called for. And kids were howling too! Sorry dear."

His ten year old daughter sighed and said "Oh daddy, what a rotten job you've got!" He smiled and kissed the top of her fair head, then went to fetch his emergency bag from the surgery at the end of the hallway. At least there was no snow to contend with.

Neither the 'garbled' address he had, nor the patient's name were familiar to him. It turned out to be in a very neat residential part of the practice area. The houses were pre-war, the kind with a round stained glass window - usually a galleon – in the front door. The gardens were immaculate; the family car gleaming on the short front drive. All middle-class respectability.

To the doctor's surprise there were two Labrador puppies – one chocolate, one black, tied to the posts either side of the wide gates. They sat and were clearly bemused and sorrowful. They had tinsel round their new-looking collars.

The front door smartly opened to the doctor's ring. He was confronted by an agitated lady furiously smoking a cigarette. There came no word of thanks or apology for interrupting his Christmas Day. Dr Fellows did not know the patient, but she looked to be in need of sedation. One hand held the cigarette, the other a glass of gin or vodka and tonic. The patient took a deep measure of her drink. Virtually speechless, she led him through to the lounge. Here two young children, a girl and an older boy, were crying profusely and noisily. A man, presumably their father, stood staring out of the French windows. Mother poured herself another large drink.

"We are all in a dire state" she screeched. To add to the 'emergency', a smell of burning turkey came from the direction of the kitchen.

"Oh dear me" Dr Fellows smiled. "Now just all try to calm down and you can tell me what has happened and who the patient is".

"We are all patients in one way or another" the lady blurted out! The doctor thought "What on earth has happened?" Then the man turned from gazing out of the windows. He had a massive black eye! Then Dr Fellows realised. It was a seasonal 'domestic'.

With his usual calm, he sat everyone down and tried, professionally, to take the heat out of the situation.

The family name was Addison and it would appear that they had just come to the area; they had been put on Dr Fellow's list by the Executive Council as he was their nearest G.P.

"Now then, tell me what all this is about, and how do you think I can help the situation?" Dr Fellows decided not to kick up a fuss about being called out, even though it was Christmas Day. To the patients a crisis had occurred and the doctor was, to them, the first source of help, however misguided this may have been.

Mr Addison tried quietly, at least, to explain. "It was I who called for a doctor" he said calmly. "And yes, my actions have clearly led to the trauma. I think we may all need a steadying word; and maybe my shocked wife would benefit from a mild sedative."

The doctor interjected "And you, Mr Addison, need me to look at that eye. Dare I ask how you came by it? You may have to let the Eye Casualty at Hospital look at it."

"I did it!" shrieked Mrs Addison bursting into tears. "Our family is not normally as volatile as this."

"But what really set off all this rumpus?" the doctor asked.

"My husband's stupidity! He knows full well that I cannot stand dogs!"

"Oh I think I see it. Is it to do with those two Labrador puppies I saw tied to the front gate?" The children burst into further tears. Mr Addison looked embarrassed. "Yes. A surprise present for the children. I made a great mistake. We had spoken of it though"

"I lost my temper and hit him" wailed Mrs Addison "what shall I do?"

"Let us all talk things over calmly" the doctor said. "Firstly Mrs Addison I suggest you go and look at your turkey, or you may have no Christmas dinner either." She dashed from the room in horror! Very fortunately all was well in the kitchen.

The Addisons turned out to be a pleasant enough family, yet typical of the kind of folk who were coming into the area. Mr Addison was a middle-manager with an old established insurance company. His wife did not have a job apart from that all-important role as 'housewife and mother'. She was certainly highly-strung, and liked to keep up appearances.

On closer examination the trauma to Mr Addison's eye was superficial, with no visual damage. Both he and his wife were reassured of this. And it transpired – as Dr Fellows suspected – the two Labrador puppies bought by Mr Addison on impulse for the family had started the rumpus. They could in no way stay under this roof, and the sooner they were re-homed the better.

Dr Fellows made the situation clear to all, then surprisingly suggested he should give Mr Addison what was initially paid for them, plus a small top-up fee, to be spent on the children (if only to stop the tears). Actually the doctor and his family had much experience of dogs over many years. It was all agreed and the cheque was written.

The doctor telephoned his wife before he left the Addisons, firstly to see if any further calls had come in (they hadn't) and to explain what he had done and just whom he was bringing home. Mrs Fellows was a stoical person quite used to her husband's often odd ways of resolving problems. His wife was a great dog lover, indeed both doctor and Mrs Fellows were still mourning the passing of a much loved dog who had been with them since before their little daughter had been born.

The Addisons were told that if ever their children wanted a walk with the dogs when they were properly trained, they – the two families – could arrange something. Frankly the doctor felt this would never transpire and it didn't.

To keep the family satisfied with their treatment, the black eye was given drops and an eye-patch to be worn for a couple of days, while Mrs Addison received half a dozen 'equanil' tablets for her 'nerves' and advised to avoid the gin for at least a couple of days. The grumpy look on her face gave the impression this would not be adhered to. Still, she would come to no harm. Dr Fellows talked sense into the children, who were surprisingly quite sensible with regard to Max and Ben 'moving on' to a new home. The doggy surprise was perhaps wearing off.

* * * *

The two puppies seemed to enjoy the ride to the Fellows' house where they were greeted with much love from the doctor's little girl. The puppies were actually brothers, and growing into fine dogs. They lived many years, like their household predecessors.

The Addisons did not stay long in the area, nor troubled the doctor again as patients, but they always sent a card at Christmas. Only once did Mrs Fellows reply, three or so years later, enclosing an up-to-date photograph of their daughter with Max and Ben, all now growing happily.

Dedicatory footnote: 'In loving memory of Max, Ben and Sandy, plus Jessie from an earlier time.' SM

1971 – Archibald's Day Out

August Bank Holiday

Edith awoke and lay enjoying the sounds of a new morning. Soon she would start to get up and go, albeit stiffly, downstairs to make her morning cup of tea, take her tablets, then listen to the radio until her elderly joints moved with a little more ease.

The day promised welcome sunshine and warmth. Lucky, for it was the Bank Holiday. Folk would be off to the sea-side or into the countryside. A break from the trauma of town life.

Edith considered the traffic jams and steaming chaos that the day would undoubtedly bring to the roads. She was relieved she had no such plans for journeying.

On the local radio station Edith heard the early news, becoming interested in the local events happening that day. The Presenter – Danny Grant – chatted away with his usual enthusiasm. And one item did catch her attention. Danny's persuasive tones made it sound quite important. That afternoon there was to be a 'Teddy Bear's picnic' held in the gardens of the local Health Authority Headquarters. The entrance fee of one pound fifty pence would go to leukaemia research; in fact the whole afternoon was devoted to that worthy cause. The idea of a 'Teddy Bear's picnic' was a gimmick; a bit of fun to draw the crowds. Children and adults were asked to bring along their favourite Teddy bears to sit with their proud owners while the picnic was enjoyed. At the end of the afternoon a competition would be held to find the best looking Teddy, the oldest Teddy and so on.

After her breakfast Edith was still thinking about the Teddy bear's picnic. She knew the venue well. The building that now housed the Health Authority had originally been a Children's Hospital. Now this had transferred to a new teaching hospital on the edge of town. Edith thought that at this time of year the gardens would be a delight. What a lovely day out it would be for people. She hoped the attendance would be big, for such a good cause.

The more Edith thought about it, the more she had the urge herself to go along. Why shouldn't she? And she would take Archibald along with her. Would it look so silly, an old lady and an old Teddy bear? Surely not. Teddy Bears were for life!

Looking into the tin on the mantelshelf, Edith assessed the financial possibilities of the idea. One pound fifty pence entrance fee, plus any extras represented quite a lot of money in her book. The tin contained three pounds and forty two pence. It was not intended for any particular purpose – just 'rainy day' money. So why shouldn't it become 'sunny day' money' and be used for a little pleasure? Edith planned her afternoon.

The first thing she did was to take an envelope and jot down a list of things to do. She would have to think carefully about the preparation of her simple picnic. Just a few sardine sandwiches, biscuits and a slice of fruit cake. To drink she could take a flask of tea, or perhaps a bottle of her homemade lemonade. That would do. On top of the envelope she wrote ARCHIBALD in capital letters. In fact the whole afternoon rather depended on Archibald's availability for the function. Could he be found easily? How would he look now?

The stairs to the attic seemed extra steep. As she opened the door, morning sunshine flooded through the big sky-light. The musty room was already hot. For a moment Edith sat looking at all the boxes and other items that were stored up here out of the way. Much had rested here for the entire sixty years she had occupied the house. An attic with sixty years of memory. Archibald had shared such memories. He was indeed a part of them.

Directly under the skylight was a large old-fashioned trunk with brass fittings. Edith got up and with difficulty from arthritic finger joints, managed to undo the catches. The lid creaked open. Spread over the contents of the trunk was a thick layer of old newspaper, the top being dated September 1938. Had it really been so long since the trunk was packed? It had. And somewhere in there, safe and sound, through war and peace, Archibald had rested for 33 years, for it was now 1971.

Edith removed the old newspapers and carefully looked at various items. All were individually wrapped in tissue paper. Reaching down into one corner Edith removed a bulky object of indeterminate shape and gently pulled off the wrapping.

Sitting on another box Edith smiled at Archibald. His fur was worn, especially on his ears. One arm hung limply by his side, but the old face was as happy as ever it had been, and in the sunlight the fine eyes shone as brightly as the day she had first held him in her arms. He was a very noble Teddy bear. The best of bears Edith thought. He had been a trusted friend since her childhood. Of course she knew the reason for his long stay in the trunk and tears filled her eyes. Then, pulling herself together, she said to him "Come on dearest Archibald, let's spruce you up my lad. I will brush your fur and then find you a bow tie. We are going out."

* * * *

Just before 1.30 Edith picked up her bags, one containing the picnic tea and the other, a large carrier bag, held Archibald, who was now dusted down and resplendent in a spotted bow tie.

Fortunately there was only one bus ride to make and their destination was close to the bus stop. Edith did not fancy walking far as the day grew hot. She had in mind a shady spot in the gardens. Hopefully they had not changed too much over the years.

Edith Moore had lived in the city all her life. Now everywhere she looked there was change. Not all to the good either. As for Archibald, he had come from a big department store in the city centre on Christmas Eve 1914. A very special present for the then five year old Edith. Special because her dear father had brought him home just two days before he had marched away to do his bit for King and country in the recently started Great War. Edith never saw him again. Archibald was all that she had to remember a kind, loving father.

She stood, bags in hands, looking towards the entrance of the Health Authority Headquarters. The gates were unchanged, except for the notice. The shady drive up to the main entrance had not changed either. A route she had taken many times, each time with a different sense of anticipation. She desperately hoped the spot in the gardens she knew of had not been altered. Supposing they had built a car park upon it? Heaven forbid.

The event had attracted a large crowd. And Archibald was in good company. Teddies of all shapes, sizes and ages were arriving in the arms of proud owners.

Paying the entrance fee Edith paused and removed Archibald from his bag. He produced admiring comments from folk standing close. Suddenly Edith felt relaxed. At home with all the Teddy owners like herself. Doubtless all the Teddy bears could tell equal tales of love and devotion; of precious secrets spoken in their worn ears.

Once into the grounds Edith looked for one particular pathway, to the right of the main drive. And it was still there, and so was the beech tree, though larger now, with a seat beneath. Edith was surprised how little had changed. So, in this quiet part of the gardens Edith settled, Archibald at her side.

She would rest awhile, perhaps have a welcome cup of tea, then she would make her way across to where the main activity of the event was taking place. Edith thought it would be fun to enter Archibald for the 'Oldest Teddy' competition, but it was of small moment if she was too late for this. The other bit of excitement she promised herself was a visit to the Local Radio tent. It would be lovely to see the 'voices' she knew so well. Hopefully Danny Grant would be there. Edith would try and have a brief word with him, just to say "hello".

After a rest in the welcome shade Edith felt relaxed. It was good that here in these pleasant surroundings the chaotic world appeared to have stood still awhile. She could just sit and enjoy her thoughts and the inevitable memories. And she was with Archibald. It was a comfort to have him at her side. Then along came two Brownies.

For a moment the little girls stood and looked at the old lady with her Teddy bear. Like all such children they whispered and giggled nervously, but clearly they wanted to approach her. One Brownie clutched a book of raffle tickets. Presumably they were trying to sell these for a good cause; working for their 'Brownie points.' Edith smiled at them. Two happy, fresh-faced little girls in their brown and yellow uniforms, their sashes adorned with badges gained for this and that project. They came closer.

"Excuse me. Would you like to buy a raffle ticket for the Grand Draw?" The girl who did the talking was a pretty little thing. Fair hair and serious grey eyes. Her friend, equally pretty with long dark hair and dark eyes, joined in the persuasion.

"The tickets are only ten pence each; or fifty pence a book. There are some great prizes." All the while she was studying Archibald. "You have a lovely Teddy. Is he very old?"

Edith smiled at the wide-eyed innocence of the pair. "Yes he is my dears. Archibald is 57 years old. Nearly as old as I am." She laughed, and the Brownies giggled even more. Edith agreed to have a book of tickets. It felt good to be giving to such a worthwhile cause. And she liked these little Brownies. The dark haired one, with her lovely eyes, reminded Edith of another little girl. In fact the resemblance was uncanny. Archibald would have thought so too. Maybe she was reading more into it than was true, but there was a definite likeness.

The fair haired Brownie was also curious about Archibald.

"How long have you actually had your Teddy?" she asked. But her friend tried to stop the interrogation from going too far.

"Don't be so nosey Louise" she hissed. Edith laughed at them.

"I don't mind your questions. To tell the truth this is the first outing poor old Archibald has had for very many years. I was given him when I was five years old. Then for a while, before the last war, he was loved by someone else." The Brownies were a little puzzled at all this history, but they were truly fascinated by Archibald.

"He has very long arms" remarked the dark haired girl, whose name was Helen.

"Yes, and he has a little hump at the top of his back" Louise observed. "Does that show how old he is?"

Edith thought how nice it was to have such interest shown in her again.

"I believe that is so." she smiled. "He was a new bear in 1914." The little girls looked thoughtful, doing a calculation.

"If your Teddy is 57 years old then he is as old as our Brownie movement. Do you know we were called 'Rosebuds' before Brownies?"

"How interesting. But do you know when your own pack was formed?" Edith asked. She had her own reasons for the question. Louise and Helen shook their heads, yet kept stroking Archibald's old fur. Or lack of it!

"I don't really know" answered Louise, continuing "but I think Miss Rhodes will. She is our Brown Owl." They were so deep in conversation they did not notice the arrival of two other people.

"What will Brown Owl know?" asked a pleasant voice. The girls jumped up, rather embarrassed that Brown Owl had caught them chatting rather than selling their raffle tickets. Edith felt she must speak up for them.

"The girls are keeping me very good company, and have a great interest in my old Teddy bear. I'm Mrs Moore by the way. We were wondering when your particular Brownie pack was formed?"

Brown Owl was a bonny lady. The elderly gentleman with her was her father. He was a retired doctor and had been a Consultant at the Children's Hospital. He didn't look as old as his ninety-one years, and still had an alert and kindly twinkle in his eyes. Hilary Rhodes began to explain.

"Our pack, the 1st Parkside, was formed in 1926. It will be forty five years old next month. One of the oldest in the area."

"Are you having any form of celebration to mark the anniversary?" Edith enquired.

"Yes, there is a little birthday party planned" Hilary Rhodes replied. Edith then made her suggestion. It took courage.

"I wonder if… I mean, as the girls like Archibald so much…I wonder if you would like him to come along as, say, the pack mascot. Just for a bit of fun. What do you think?"

The two Brownies jumped for joy. "Oh Brown Owl do please say he can come!"

"That is most kind of you Mrs Moore. A lovely idea. But are you sure? He looks to be rather a valuable bear. And a pack of little girls can be rather boisterous."

"He is valuable certainly. But I'm sure they will take care of him. I do have a good reason for my offer." Edith paused. In a few minutes all this meeting and talk had been quite remarkable. Quite unexpected. She had suddenly recalled something important from the past. Names had fallen into place, yet for the moment only Edith appreciated this, or so she felt. It was all rather delightful, if poignant. Then came the surprise. Old Dr Rhodes had said little, but clearly enjoyed all the enthusiasm going on about him. Then he quietly remarked, "You may think this odd, but I am sure I have seen this particular Teddy before. He has such a special look about him."

Hilary Rhodes laughed. "Oh father, you must have seen many hundreds of teddies in your time. Little children always cling to something familiar for comfort when they are patients."

"I agree Hilary dear. Yet I am certain this old chap and I have met before. What is more, I believe our meeting was beneath this very tree." Edith then knew her own belief and recollection had been correct.

"We have met before Dr Rhodes. Only there were three of us then. Myself, Archibald and a little girl. She was your patient at the time. You were so kind to us. In so many years it's only dear Archibald here that hasn't changed."

Dr Rhodes sat down beside Edith and took her hands. "Yes I do remember your little girl. A pretty child with a mop of dark hair and big eyes. A bit like Helen here" he chuckled. Helen, despite her young age managed a blush. "Am I right?" he asked. Edith nodded and felt the tears well up in her eyes.

"What a memory you must have Doctor. Dorothy, Archibald and I used to come and sit here under this tree, weather and Ward Sister permitting. This was our favourite place. I am surprised it is still here and just the same." She turned to Louise and Helen, now very quiet.

"You see girls this is why Archibald is so special. Not just because he was my Teddy and I loved him very much, but because he was also loved by my daughter. She was a Brownie. And by coincidence she was in your Pack. I well remember the evening she stood and made her 'Brownie promise'. Such a serious little face, but so full of enthusiasm and life." Edith's words faltered and she dipped into her bag for a hanky. Doctor Rhodes put an arm around her. "I understand my dear" he said quietly.

Of course it had to happen. Louise, wide-eyed and so innocent continued to probe the matter.

"Mrs Moore, can your daughter Dorothy bring Archibald to our Pack party?"

Doctor Rhodes, knowing the full story, looked a shade uncomfortable. Edith had been half prepared for this moment and the inevitable question which she would not avoid. Of course she would tell the child everything. No harm in her understanding.

"I'm afraid that won't be possible my dear. You see, Dorothy died of leukaemia only a few months after making that 'Brownie promise'. That is the reason I came here this afternoon. We both knew this garden so well."

"I think you were very brave" said Louise solemnly. It is amazing how often little girls come out with the right remark at the right time. Edith smiled.

"Well it did take a bit of courage to face the memories. But we wanted to do our bit for the charity. So worthwhile. And you mustn't be sad, because they can do so much more for little children with leukaemia now, as I am sure Doctor Rhodes would be able to explain better than I. And do you know, this is the first outing poor old Archibald has had since Dorothy died."

"It's a long time indoors" said Helen.

"It is indeed, years too long" Edith laughed.

"I'm sorry for asking." Louise tried to apologise. Edith put a fond arm about her. "Don't worry my dear. This has been a wonderful afternoon for both myself and Archibald. A fresh beginning for him, sweet old thing. And I know he will like being admired and loved again. Thank you all for that." And she hugged the Teddy bear in a way she had not done for years.

1973 – The Meeting

(A light hearted glimpse of an attempt at health education in a country General Practice during the early 1970s)

The villages of Upper and Lower Grinding defied current trends and showed a marked increase in the birth rate. Whether due to repeated breakdowns at a local electricity sub-station, or to the final disappearance of the mobile cinema is purely academic, but the situation did cause grave alarm. Those most affected – apart from the expecting parties – were Dr Wilfred Wellbeloved O.B.E., Chairman of the Parochial Church Council, prize winning rose grower and general practitioner (in that order). And more directly, Nurse Muriel Joy, midwife, confidant and High Anglican, who had been semi-retired since 1950, and with remarkable ease had managed to resist all efforts to keep up to date. As most of her patients were to all intents 'private', in that the Local Authority appeared to have no knowledge of them or share in them, Nurse Joy thrived on tradition, goodwill and good luck! She had hardly left the village in forty years, and the only memory of her London training was of being entertained to tea at the Dorchester, but sadly letting the side down by asking for a cup of Bovril. Despite many failings the mothers adored her; Dr Wellbeloved needed her, and all had run smoothly for years.

This awesome partnership was now faced with so many babies yelling or about to yell in nearly every home, that it seemed reasonable to conclude some form of education was needed, not simply to prepare the mothers to be, but to provide them with the necessary information on how to avoid the business again. While Nurse Joy was the usual advisor on such personal matters as constipation, piles, 'the curse' and 'the change', Dr Wellbeloved was privately uncertain of her ability in this particular sphere, being a most maiden of maiden ladies, and especially as it was common knowledge that she had told several members of the senior Sunday school that a brothel was a Salvation Army soup kitchen!

Dr Wellbeloved enjoyed his journals. And the latest rather exciting publication to come his way was one dealing with sexual medicine. This came as a bit of a shock, but a country G.P. has to keep an open mind on these things, and if medicine need become sexual then fair enough, and lucky for some. But it was between these glossy pages that he found a reference to teaching sexual hygiene in schools, and to health education generally. Like most other hard-pressed middle aged doctors this new adjunct to preventive health (a strange misnomer if ever there was one), was something very interesting. Health education seemed a good idea in that it was obvious that if he could educate his patients to stay healthy then he would have more time with the P.C.C. and his roses. Eagerly Wellbeloved sought more literature on the subject, but the more he delved the more complicated it all seemed. At last he discovered that help was available locally where arranging classes for his patients was concerned.

Trevor Iain Thomas ('knocker Thomas' to his friends) answered his office telephone at Area Health Authority H.Q., giving an impression he was frantically involved. Actually he was sitting with his feet up on the desk munching a bacon cob and reading the Guardian, but no matter. Dr Wellbeloved's problem met with a series of intellectual grunts interspersed with the occasional 'yar', as expected from all dynamic 'in' people. The problem explained, Thomas said he could help.

"You feel" he observed, "that these pregnant mums and their husbands would really benefit from such a meeting?" Dr Wellbeloved said he thought so, and how could one go about it.

"Yar..well, we could arrange a useful day-long seminar at some local place. You know, talks, films, slides, and then break up into 'buzz groups' for discussion and evaluation."

"No, I think that would be too formal and academic. Remember my patients are mostly good honest farming folk!

Thomas removed his feet from the desk, slung aside the newspaper and his cob to launch into a verbal attack!

"Ah but you see Doctor, the expectant mother is such a vital, aware person. Her creative self is bursting with expression and concern; and while her basic personality is obviously of an inward thinking, essentially caring person, she feels a deep need to express herself as that person, but most important to positively respond to the role of mother, child bearer and intrinsically sexually satisfied woman!"

There was silence from the other end of the line. Dr Wellbeloved was for once speechless!

"On the other hand" continued Thomas, "I could arrange to show some films."

It sounded a more acceptable idea, but where and when?

"We have a choice of two films actually. There is 'To Doris a Daughter' and a later, more modern version – 'Ready for Herbert'. This is very valuable, as it demonstrates the role of the father and his social participation in the birth."

This last film was definitely not suitable as Nurse Joy refused to have any father within miles of a confinement. Anyway the men would not wish to be there for a very good reason. It was an unspoken arrangement that Nurse paid for every pint her fathers cared to drink during this time – but in a pub three miles away at Middle Wollup. She would even loan her bicycle so they could get there. It was a form of tradition to be seen 'riding Nurse's bike' - a signal to the village that the happy event was near. So 'Ready for Herbert' was definitely out.

"We'll show 'Doris' then" replied Thomas. "Where can the meeting be held?"

"At my place" said Wellbeloved.

"In the waiting area I presume?"

"The sitting room actually." Another silence fell.

"Wouldn't the waiting area be more suitable? I mean for space and seating availability etc."

"No. My waiting room is not quite right." Dr Wellbeloved never spoke a truer word. The waiting room was approximately 12' x 5' and took the form of a lean-to shed attached to the surgery. For nearly two centuries patients had made do with this and even the sudden innovation of health education within the practice was not sufficient cause to change things. So the sitting room it would be – at his own risk – and with the formal consent of Mrs Wellbeloved.

In due course all the expectant parents were briefed by Nurse Joy, doubtless with veiled threats of castor oil and soft soap enemas should they not attend.

Came the night, the earnest Trevor Thomas duly arrived accompanied by a spotty youth called Frank – the expert on film projection. Together they swiftly transformed the sitting room into a cinema, adeptly swinging cables and equipment into the most unlikely places. At last all was ready.

"Will you manage to get them all in?" enquired Thomas, politely sipping the dry sherry the Doctor had given him.

"I would think so, but there may be a lot. Nurse Joy has her methods of persuasion".

Nurse had been given Mrs Wellbeloved's blessing to invite whom she wished, and the result was fruitful to say the least! Up the drive they marched. Eighteen expectant mothers of all shapes and sizes; their supporting spouses, relatives and pets producing a rear-guard effect – a force hardly to be reckoned with. How they all managed to find a space facing the screen was amazing, but they did and the show began.

Two things were obvious from Trevor Thomas' opening remarks. First, the audience hadn't a notion of what he was on about, and second, he seemed anxious about the effect of the film. He tentatively asked if they all realised what they were about to see, a question which produced a most vulgar reply from the practice's record-holding multipara. Unscathed, Thomas pressed home his health education for all the 'ladies in waiting', but added the proviso that if anyone did feel a little woozy during the birth sequences they should beat a hasty retreat. This produced more hoots of mirth and a brief spate of betting as to who would be the first to go.

The film proved a saga as powerful as 'Gone with the Wind'. The audience was silent apart from the repetitive crunching of popcorn and peanuts. No-one showed the slightest embarrassment at the generous proportions of Doris, shot in a variety of indelicate positions. They did not fit, faint or vomit at the emergence of the daughter. No, it was a model meeting. As the last of the credits flickered away and the lights came on there was silence; but everyone looked happy. Trevor Thomas gave Dr Wellbeloved a smug grin and remarked "Yar, I think they were terribly involved, don't you?" Before he could reply there came from the back of the room the raucous tones of Mrs Mavis Crabtree, Lower Grinding's most trusted barmaid. She addressed her husband, the dyspeptic Ronald.

"Eh luv, 'av you got that crate of ale? I don't know about t'others but I'm in a reet muck sweat!" Obviously an inward thinking, essentially caring person expressing herself! Anyway it had been fun.

Postscript: this story is dedicated to the memory of Noel Wass and John McClusky with whom I worked for many happy years in the 1970's. SM

1974 – The Farthing Breakfast

On the last November evening of 1974, Dr Eva Porter sat in her old-established branch surgery in an East Midlands town. She had just seen her last patient at her last surgery, an honour that had fallen to a little eight year old girl sent into the night, alone, to see the doctor about a chesty cough. As so often happened, no parent had bothered to accompany her – a common enough occurrence, what with society changing fast and no-one seeming to care. Eva, though, suddenly thought back to forty years ago, to the "Farthing Breakfasts" provided by those who did care.

1936. Paddington, London.

The Outpatients Casualty Room at St. Marys Hospital had been quiet throughout the night, and now two starched nurses prepared it for the day ahead. Dawn tried to make itself known through a London pea-souper fog, with the frosted glass windows already clouded up by steam from the ancient sterilisers boiling up instruments in readiness.

A nurse looked up to see, standing in the doorway, a tall thin woman and a scruffy, tearful little girl biting her lip and with a blood stained bandage on her knee. The senior nurse began to take details while despatching the duty porter to wake the Casualty Dresser, who still had an hour of duty left.

"Lucy tripped on our step as she came for her breakfast. She must have fallen on something sharp." The lady was very apologetic.

"Coming for breakfast? What do you mean? I don't understand!" The nurse was irritable and brusque. Then she saw the bonnet.

"I am from the Salvation Army Centre in Paddington" the lady explained politely. "Before they go to school, any hungry child can have a breakfast for a farthing. Just a mug of cocoa, some porridge and bread and jam. It fills empty tummies" she smiled, adding "Lucy is often first in the queue. God bless her."

The nurse asked, scribbling down notes "She hasn't had any food yet, has she?" If the child needed an anaesthetic, this could cause problems

"No, she had to have this wound seen to first" and so Lucy was placed on a hard examination couch, with her kind friend banished to the corner.

A sleepy young woman, wearing a short white coat over her jumper and tweed suit, entered the Casualty Room. In her final months as a medical student at St. Mary's, Eva Porter smiled down at the tearful silent child. She liked children and hoped to get a House job on the Paediatric ward before leaving the hospital world. She read the name on the nurse's card and set to work.

"Now Lucy dear, we'll mop you up and stitch you up like a dolly and then you can go off home. Is Mummy with you?"

Lucy pointed to the corner. Eva turned round and saw the Salvation Army lady.

"Oh! I see you brought her in. How kind."

The knee was cleaned up, with Lucy biting her grubby handkerchief when told a stitch would be needed. Eva's gentle needlework was well known in Casualty and she chatted to the little girl while doing the suturing, a practice with which some of the nurses did not agree. When she had finished, a little voice whispered "Can I go and have my farthing breakfast now, Miss?"

Eva, who had not heard the initial conversation smiled; yes of course she could have her breakfast, then asked why a "farthing breakfast"? The Salvation Army lady coughed discreetly, explaining to Eva their facility for the less fortunate children whose homes did not provide breakfast. She chose her words with the utmost care so as not to embarrass Lucy, for some children, even at that age, were told they should never accept charity. Eva was very interested, causing the nurses to raise irritated and sceptical eyebrows. She commented innocently "But surely it's not charity if they pay a farthing?"

"Not all have a farthing, but all have at least a hot drink" was the quiet reply.

She asked "Where do you hold these breakfasts?"

The lady, Mrs Good (an apt name) told her, inviting Eva to call in and see for herself.

"Do come along Doctor and see our happy café."

An hour later, off duty, Eva left her lodgings near the Medical School and made her way to Paddington's Salvation Army Centre. She observed the worn uneven steps on which Lucy had fallen and cut her knee; inside, she heard the clamour of the little diners sitting at trestle tables. There were bowls of steaming porridge, mugs of cocoa, mountains of bread and jam, all devoured with a gusto that amazed her. These were, though, hungry children, some of whom had had precious little food since the previous day's breakfast. From amid the chaos, a voice called out. It was Mrs Good. "Do come in Doctor, please. You see, we are all being sustained at last!"

At the end of one table Eva saw her patient. Lucy was eagerly clasping a big mug. There was jam all round her mouth. Seeing the Doctor, she smiled – a smile devoid of two front teeth. Turning to her neighbour, equally jammy, she said in a loud whisper and with feeling "Cor! She's the one what sewed me knee up without it 'urting! She's nice to kids, too."

Eva had never had such a compliment broadcast to so many. She felt rather humble – a good feeling, though.

Gradually the children dispersed. Mrs Good and Eva sat down to drink tea and eat fresh bread and jam.

"What do you think of our breakfast scheme, doctor?"

"I think it a most sensible and valuable idea, but I should tell you, Mrs Good, that I am not yet a doctor but just a Final Year student. I sit the exams in April."

"My dear, you are all doctors to us. You are so good with the children. Poor mites! They face terrible poverty and deprivation."

Eva remarked "At least you and your colleagues and the Salvation Army are doing something constructive. That mug of cocoa and bite to eat will have set Lucy and her friends up for the morning at least. I only see them when they fall ill and try to pick up the pieces when there is little resistance left."

Mrs Good placed a hand on Eva's arm. "That is why I beg you to drop in again if you can spare the time, for your observant eye might just spot illness in its early stage. But I am sure you will do a lot of good in your life."

Despite working for Finals, Eva made time for a farthing breakfast occasionally. It was good groundwork. She made many little friends and was comforted by Mrs Good's caring work. She qualified in April, as she had hoped and – after a couple of Hospital jobs, one with children – left London for the Midlands and an assistantship in a working-class practice.

* * * *

Eva locked her surgery door for the last time and began to walk to her car. The rain had started and the night ahead looked bleak. Then she saw little Lucy, her last patient, sitting huddled in a shop doorway. "Lucy dear, what are you doing here? You should be off home to the warm and taking your medicine!" The child smiled at her. Again two front teeth were missing. It was a smile from the past, the smile of another Lucy long ago.

"Me Mam and Dad is out, doctor. If I went 'ome I'd still 'ave to sit on the step." Eva was shocked. Surely not in this day and age…

"Did you have your tea before coming to the surgery?"

"No. Mam said she han't any cash for chips."

It was the farthing breakfast scenario, forty years on. Had nothing changed? She supposed it had, but the cause now was more indifference than circumstance. It was pay day. Mam and dad were doubtless in the pub. Eva knew she had to help, as others – like Mrs Good, of happy memory, had helped years ago, in Paddington.

"Could you eat a fish and chip supper?" she asked. Lucy looked as though she had been invited to the Savoy Grill Room.

"Yes, doctor! I've never 'ad fish!"

Ten minutes later, Eva Porter and Lucy were tucking into cod and chips in the "posh" café part of the local fish and chip shop. Eva thought to herself "I'm ending as I began." Only the mugs of cocoa were missing.

Footnote: First published in 'The Journal of the Medical Writers Society 2006-07'. SM

During the 1930's children on their way to school could buy breakfast for a farthing at the Salvation Army Centre. They had hot coco, bread, jam and porridge. Children who could not pay were given their breakfast for nothing.

In one week in 1935 over 250 children were fed at the centre.

The source of this picture is unknown, but it inspired this story.
SM

2013 – Doctor Calls it a Day

Dr Joe Foley wearily made his way into the consulting room of his practice on the edge of the town. He had been out twice during the previous evening. He still insisted on going to every urgent call up until midnight. Indeed the patients who made up his moderately sized list refrained from disturbing him in the night without a very good cause. If the telephone rang the other side of the midnight hour he knew the reason would be genuine and possibly dire. He was no partaker in the 'out of hours get-out' policy, nor had he paid money to be a part of this. Many of his list were now elderly patients. Respiratory ills, despite modern drugs, were still a problem. Left ventricular failure with pulmonary oedema were just as life-threatening as they had been when he was a young hospital physician. These were GP emergencies to his mind. He was a GP.

And the late evening, or the dead of night, had always been the time the Almighty seemed intent on calling certain members of His flock to Glory! In truth, with modern management, some of the traditional nocturnal emergencies were seen less often. Now, the elderly especially, were prone to agitation and shouting abuse at the younger members of the family at God-forsaken hours – also the doctor (or an ambulance crew) sent for to calm the nerves of them all. However, patients – or 'customers' as the ambulance service now called them - would often decide they had made a big mistake and demand to 'be released' when the professionals had carried out all their string of tests to make sure all at least appeared satisfactory. A release was only disallowed if it was an overdose, those found to actually have heart problems following chest pain, or indeed somebody with a very high blood pressure or 'transient ichaemic attack', no matter how 'mini'!

Despite it being mid-Winter, that day things were singularly quiet, and when evening surgery began at 5pm the waiting room was nearly empty. Even so Dr Foley still preferred to hold 'open surgeries' as of old. No-one complained, because one was usually certain of being seen in due course. Foley was most surely the last doctor in the area to still work in this way and his list size easily allowed for it, as it always had.

The following day was his arranged day off, and he had that morning an appointment with the television! During the previous evening's surgery one of his regular patients came to tell him that the next scheduled programme would be of interest to him. Surprisingly the son of the patient together with his girlfriend (or more fashionably called 'partner' – she was neither fiancée nor married to him) were to be the centre of attention on what was titled 'The Jeremy Kyle show' where personal problems were aired, and after a suitable 'berating', assessment and advice would be freely given. Indeed, Dr Foley would be very relieved if someone would give the young man, Darren, his lady, and indeed the whole bloody family some needed advice they would heed! Foley felt there was but faint chance of this, for they were not the kind of folk that would heed anything that did not come from the lips of a Crown Court Judge, if that!

Turning to the under-used TV the doctor watched as its picture closed in on a group on the platform – the young couple seated (or rather slouched) in comfortable chairs. The presenter/host was a youngish, well-groomed man who had no chair but for some reason chose to crouch before them as if about to spring onto their joint laps. It was all a bit bizarre. And the noisy dialogue between all parties reached high decibels, such was its fury and invective. Darren and his partner were clearly unhappy about the joint care of a child which Dr Foley had never heard mentioned. He silently thanked his Maker that they had moved off his list when they 'set up home'. It was clearly not a happy domicile.

The telephone suddenly shrilled out and as this was also his willing receptionist/secretary Marilyn's day off, he took the call and drew towards him a note pad. The caller, the local police, had one of his patients in custody for a usual offence of begging up at the shops, and contending he was really 'Jesus Christ in need of a bite!' Dr Foley agreed to come along and calm things down as the troubled man was in fact an old university friend, with many ills and problems.

The Doctor's vintage Wolsey 1500 pulled into the police car park where, as usual, its shiny, distinctive dove-grey and Cardinal red trim with a walnut and leather interior, drew the motoring enthusiasts from both the police officers and especially the mechanics from the garage. This gem from the early 1960s was in remarkable condition, and was said never to have let the doctor down when he had an emergency. The amazing fact was that he had originally purchased it from a veterinary surgeon who only ever kept his 'new car' for six months!

An office door opened and a WPC came toward the old boy with a smile on her face. They were great friends.

"I'm afraid it's your old pal 'the Vicar' again. He started to get a bit stroppy; even pulled rank on us!"

"Oh is he Jesus today, or John the Baptist?" Foley tried not to laugh, but this, probably his only psychiatric patient, because he was anti-medication, was a genuine bloody nuisance. He could also 'flash' at complaining old ladies when he was annoyed. Strangely the only person who could calm him down, apart from Dr Foley, was the WPC, whose name was Shelley. He had once mentioned to her that she was like his older sister from years back. Dr Foley could remember a sister who had been introduced to him at a Cambridge 'May Ball' when the man, whom he would address as 'Gilbert' was a pleasant, chummy student, reading mathematics at Pembroke. He was also an 'Exhibitioner' (such was the irony) but why had he got Jesus so much on his mind? Joe Foley still could not really understand. Walking into the spartan cell, he saw Gilbert still wore a very grubby Cambridge University tie. It had egg down it. The interview did not proceed well.

Dr Foley tried so very hard to get through to Gilbert. He first tried plain talking with references to past and hopefully happier times at Cambridge. Something they could both recall, at least he hoped so. Instantly Foley knew that he was on the wrong track. Talk and indeed all memory of University days was clearly a 'no-go' topic. Nor did he like Gilbert's change of mood. He became morose and even abusive to the doctor whom he had initially looked upon as an old friend. This had all gone.

After a bit more of this unsatisfactory situation and getting nowhere, Dr Foley decided to telephone a private psychiatric hospital with whom previous patients had seemed to fare well. The senior medical officer on duty gladly agreed to take this distressed man in for assessment and any emergency care deemed necessary.

Replacing the telephone receiver, Foley felt that while this was not ideal management, it was really the best 'emergency measures' available these days with so many cut-backs, changes and sheer messing about, largely due to staffing problems, not to mention all the usual NHS red tape. However, what the good friend and doctor did not know as he saw Gilbert into an ambulance, was that this was the last time they would meet. Come to think about it, he never found out about Gilbert's link with 'Jesus'.

* * * *

When all was sorted out with regard to the Police paperwork generated by Gilbert's bizarre behaviour, the doctor left his Constabulary friend and headed for home. He felt very weary and fed-up on the way. Although it should not have troubled him, the business with Gilbert most certainly did, and not just because he was an old friend. When he thought about it, Dr Foley was seeing many more cases of failing mental health than in years past; and society seemed to be helping them less, with fewer caring professionals for 'back-up' when things went wrong, as all too often they did.

Once in the quiet of home, Joe Foley found that his kindly 'daily woman', Mrs Gloria Plethoridge, had certainly 'done' for him, and also left a sandwich lunch prepared, which could be readily eaten when time permitted. Picking up his mail which had come in late, he took everything through to the freshly polished dining room. He would have to watch out for breadcrumbs, or he would be reprimanded the next day!

* * * *

The postman's bundle of mail contained the usual mixture of items, though he noticed there were not so many 'hospital reports', which nowadays tended to be e-mails, picked up in Marilyn's province, as she worked the 'bloody computer', poor girl. True to say Dr Foley preferred the old record cards in battered buff envelopes!

There was a fair bit of mail on this particular day, but soon the doctor sorted it into separate piles. Fortunately not so many bills, but too much bumf and diktats from various holes of NHS administration, together with PCT nonsense, yet he thought they had been done away with, to be replaced by another crowd of 'half-wits'. Then he took hold of an envelope that was both menacing and bulky. He ripped it open like an unwanted bank statement. Here was a bundle of papers relating to a proposed 'Revalidation of his G.P. skills'. Joe Foley noted the message that this would be done before a given date in the New Year. Obviously he, and presumably various friends and colleagues, would all come in for this intrusive scrutiny!

Later, in the early evening Joe Foley went to rest awhile in a quiet, former dressing room on the landing. To some it might be thought a bit bare and unattractive. To Joe Foley it offered peace and tranquillity, ideal for an afternoon nap. Here the doctor could take necessary repose away from the irritations and worries thrown at him during the day. On this particular occasion he had slipped into something of a reverie. He was thinking back to his youth and family.

Joe Foley had been born into a long established medical family in 1939, just prior to the outbreak of the Second World War. His father, two uncles, grandfather and even great-grandfather going back to the 1830s were all in their time medical practitioners. And all bar one were educated and trained at a minor public school, then Gonville & Caius College Cambridge and after October 1854, St. Mary's Hospital new Medical School in Paddington. All seemed to later favour family practice, in London or in the depths of the English countryside. Sadly Joe did not get to know his father very well. He became a Naval Surgeon-Commander, and putting his practice into the hands of his brother Clarence, sailed away to the Battle of the Atlantic, with sad consequences!

* * * *

At this juncture Dr Foley's reverie and meanderings through youthful days promptly ceased, for work was to hand, with the ringing of an old bell which suddenly came from within a short passage leading to the surgery. In years past this had been the 'Night Bell', activated from the patient's entrance, and would be used in nocturnal emergencies after hours. Foley had not heard this ring for some considerable time, so the caller must be an old patient.

Switching on the light over the surgery door he hurried to open it, to find a man and his wife, Mr and Mrs Taylor, with their son, a child of 10, all clearly distressed. The son, Simon, had it seemed fallen ill on the bus home from school. He was more upset at having been sick on the top deck and receiving some unkind rebuke from the driver/attendant in charge. He had been put off the bus a couple of stops from home, and on arrival could only explain a little of how he felt. It was a most violent headache made worse by strong light that was the most disturbing symptom.

Once in the orderly surgery Dr Foley used the minimum of direct light with which to examine the boy. There was also marked fever and lassitude and more vomiting. A key test had to be carried out. Placing the boy on his examination couch, the Doctor took Simon's nearest leg and flexed the hip to 90 degrees. Then he went on to attempt to straighten it again. In doing so there occurred a spasm of the hamstrings, the acute pain causing Simon to cry out. A positive Kernig's sign! For this Dr Foley apologised to the boy, then quietly said "Sorry old son, I'm afraid it is hospital for you".

Very quietly the Doctor explained that this was clearly a case of meningitis and Simon must be taken over to St. Mary's Hospital for examination and assessment by the paediatricians. He then picked up the telephone receiver and dialled a number well known to him. When it was answered, he introduced himself and asked for the Paediatric SHO or Registrar on duty. As always Dr Foley tended to use the old 'grades' which did not please the young lady, presumably a staff nurse or a Sister…although these days it could have been anyone to take the call.

Very fortunately, Dr Foley's house and surgery were but a stone's throw away from the hospital. He knew the area so well he suggested that he should carry the lad round to A&E in his arms while Mr and Mrs Taylor took their car to the main car park. They had driven quite a way to the surgery that evening. So this was how the young Simon appeared before the Reception Counter, in his G.P's strong arms. If only the welcome had been more worthy of that fine hospital, some 156 years after its opening to receive the sick and injured in the Paddington District. Dr Foley approached a young lady, introduced himself and asked for the Departmental Sister in Charge. He explained he was a G.P. and had recently phoned to ask for medical help to receive the boy. Simon emphasised his plight by vomiting again. To his distress, they were told to go and wait until called. Thus Foley pulled rank, but the girl's blank face snarled, even though she continued to rhythmically chew gum throughout the discussion!

Dr Foley was most troubled by his reception at the A&E Dept. Despite the position being politely explained, no-one on the so-called Reception desk even tried to help. Just then however, help thankfully arrived in the form of a steady yet gentle hand on his shoulder. The old doctor turned round, still with Simon in his arms, to see another lapel badge level with his field of vision. The badge told all who read it that this person was no less than Professor Sir Adam Johnston, Professor of Paediatric Medicine. And many years back he had been a young House Officer attached to the Paediatric Unit, when Joe Foley was a Registrar with a Diploma in Child Health. The Consultant did recognise his old senior colleague.

Adam Johnston quickly gave orders, brisk and with great authority. A trolley appeared from heaven-knows-where; thus Simon was surrounded with St. Mary's care, much to the relief of his parents who by then had arrived in the right place.

Dr Foley introduced the Professor to Mr & Mrs Taylor, at the same time hoping no problems would worsen matters. They did not. Dr Foley soon after said goodbye to the staff and his patients. He thanked God that Adam Johnston had appeared to get things moving before the worst crisis happened. "Damn that girl" he said to himself as he strode home through the Paddington rain.

Postscript: Paddington – the day after.

Dr Foley realised that he had to unwind before going to bed that evening. He relaxed in front of a good fire, and sipped a whisky and soda – so much better than nitrazepam – more enjoyable. Something to savour, offering gradual relaxation, yet no thick head in the morning – if, of course, taken in moderation. He dozed for a while, then the telephone wakened him. It was his old friend Adam Johnston. As ever, a courtesy call to let him know that his diagnosis had been spot-on, and his action had saved the boy's life. The Prof. then suggested they meet one evening for a quiet dinner at his club in St. James's. Dr Foley agreed. It would do him good.

At 2.30 the following morning he experienced a crushing retro-sternal pain, combined with a cold sweat. His pulse felt ok when he first felt it, but soon became 'thready' and weak. The chest pain radiated to the left shoulder and inner aspect of the same arm. Joe Foley tried to keep calm and remember all the platitudes he had over the years made to his own patients when they had presented thus. He called the Deputising Service. The phone seemed to ring for an age. Then the call was answered by a sleepy female voice. The operator clearly knew her job, yet did not have reassuring news for the doctor. All the medic 'on-call' cars were busy with other sick people. Could he ring a doctor friend? Or perhaps, if he thought it truly urgent, get through to the London Ambulance Service? Dr Foley said he would be glad if some doctor became 'free' and could still come to him stat!

The Ambulance Service were quick to answer, and could tell this was serious, though at first thought Dr Foley was asking them to go to a 'chest pain cause' case. Foley managed to put them right, stressing he was alone, but would have to try to get to the door. The call activated, he headed for the stairs but paused to vomit on the landing. He finally managed to unlock both front and back doors, then slumped to the floor, hardly breathing. He had hoped his own thoughts of a silent myocardial infarction – treatable if recognised early – would be correct, which it may well have been some hours previously. When the ambulance crew opened the door and found the old man. He was beyond all help. Of course nobody knew Dr Foley was hypertensive and had been so for years. He had been treating himself, and done this very successfully, but left no notes. Of course he did not fool the Pathologist in due course!

Author's footnote

There has never to my belief been a Professor of Paediatrics with the name Sir Adam Johnston at St. Mary's Hospital in Paddington, London W2.

By 2010 St. Mary's Hospital at Paddington had a specialist Accident and Emergency unit for both children and adults, and was also a Regional Centre for the immediate treatment of Meningitis in London and the South east.

All the characters in this story are fictional.

Epilogue

The first president of the College of General Practitioners (now the Royal College) was, when it came into being in 1952, Dr W. N. Pickles of Aysgarth – probably the most distinguished country doctor of our time.

William Pickles was an example to one and all, and a leader in the field of Epidemiology. One of his sayings remains in my mind and I would commend it to all new GP's (I paraphrase…) "go into the homes of your patients and see how they live. Put on your boots and join them at work in the fields…." this of course is a sure way to get to know with what the doctor is faced – "before making a diagnosis".

Today a five minute surgery consultation to meet a 'target' is an insult to patient and doctor alike. Nothing takes the place of a patient manner, personal touch and observation as used by the 'all-rounder' of family practice.

About the Author

Stephen Morris was 'drawn' to matters medical in 1948 at the age of seven. This was brought about when his stepmother, a locum dispenser, took him to work with her at a City Mental Hospital. This grim setting led to his appointment of 'Cork Counter and Fitter' and his first hospital appointment. It was only in later life Morris appreciated, looking back, how close he had once been to dangerous drugs on one side and noises of lunacy on the other side beyond the locked dispensary door!

In the early 1960s after 12 years of hospital work (and no mum to guide him) Morris eventually ended up in a casualty department researching into the aspects of drug overdoses.

In the autumn of 1963 he had a paper published in a specialist medical Journal. It was well received and even mentioned in the national press of the day! Now 50 years on with a great many articles, short stories, books and TV work, his writing, both medical and lay, is still well researched, received, but above all most reasonable.